THE DIRT IN OUR SKIN

THE DIRT IN OUR SKIN

A NOVEL

J. J. ANSELMI

RARE BIRD
LOS ANGELES, CALIF.

READ OR DIE

THIS IS A GENUINE RARE BIRD BOOK

Rare Bird Books
6044 North Figueroa Street
Los Angeles, CA 90042
rarebirdbooks.com

Copyright © 2024 by JJ Anselmi

TRADE PAPERBACK ORIGINAL EDITION

For more information, address:
Rare Bird Books Subsidiary Rights Department
6044 North Figueroa Street
Los Angeles, CA 90042

Set in Dante
Printed in the United States

10 9 8 7 6 5 4 3 2 1

Library of Congress Cataloging-in-Publication Data available upon request

For Stevie and Ida.
Also, TBC will never die.

Prologue

When we're out here, we're together. The dirt, our chains, the trees—these are the things that bind us. We know these lines like we know each other, like we know the contours of our bodies. The lips and landings rise triumphantly from the ground, monuments to the woods and soil that protect us. Our jumps flow between the trees in ways the land decided on long ago, chutes leading to something larger than ourselves.

When we're out here, we don't find much reason to talk. Instead molding and carving the dirt in quiet, stolid determination, molding and carving it into something it was meant to be—but that wouldn't exist if it weren't for our hands, shovels, and wheelbarrow. Someday, the land will reclaim its soil, swallowing what we've created to feed the trees, vines, and worms.

We'll still be here.

If the sounds of our tools working the soil aren't in the air, it's the sound of our tires, that sweet, buzzing zip; it's the sawblade roar of our freewheels, cutting through the land, not in conquest but in communion, and, sometimes, it's the sound of the tree branches reaching out to touch our shoulders like old friends as we emulate the deliberate, cutting flight of the hawks and owls.

We've spent countless hours building, but that doesn't feel quite right to say because time doesn't exist out here, not in the same way. The old path started as a walking trail, rows of tobacco beyond the tree line. But what's here now—three interwoven chutes from which our work arises like naturally occurring EKG lines—seems as ancient as the dirt itself. You can soar between the lines; you can charge through each individual one. There are so many different possibilities. Even if you stick to one line, there are shark fins, rollers, hips, and berms—because straight jumps bore the shit out of us.

PART ONE

Boys of Summer

1

Knocked unconscious, blood spilled down my face from a gash just above my hairline. When I came to, Jason had me in his arms. Drill bits of pain bored through my skull. Telling the story years later, Jason would sarcastically say, "You would've died if I wasn't there. Do you realize that? You owe me your life." But that's really how I saw it.

We'd been riding our newly built dirt jumps in the woods that split the distance between my house and his. Jason's dad was a tobacco farmer. Our jumps butted up against their sprawling field and its sweet-smelling plants. My parents' property was only a few acres away.

"Let's do a train," Jason had said.

I followed him as closely as I could without touching his tire with mine. The last thing I remember clearly: him blasting off the lip and cranking an X-up[1] farther than he ever had, twisting his arms and turning his front tire almost ninety degrees past his frame.

"Holy shit!" I yelled.

Amazed by what I'd seen, my attention drifted away from my own bike for a split second, and then I got tense and pushed down too hard into the landing. My front wheel cased the packed dirt with an ugly clank. I got sent over my handlebars, flying for a moment before smashing my face into a tree trunk.

1   Turn to page 244 for a BMX glossary.

Waking up, I felt like someone had crushed my head in a table vice. I covered my head in my arms and tucked my knees against my chest, moaning. This went on for a few minutes before Jason said, "We gotta get you to the hospital."

I stood up but immediately felt dizzy, weak on my feet. The glaring sunlight was an explosion behind my eyes. "What about our bikes?" I asked.

"Who cares? You're bleeding out of your head." He turned around and kneeled. "I'll carry you on my back."

Jason was wearing a white T-shirt. I left blood splotches on his shoulder as I held on. He trudged forward on a mission, bracing my butt with his hands as we made our way through the woods and then his dad's field. He walked one foot in front of the other, mindful, even during an emergency, not to fuck up his dad's tobacco plants. The field reached out in every direction, seeming much larger than ever before. Jason sweated in the summer sun. My hands became slick on his neck.

His dad, Scott, was in the front yard, fixing his old tractor. That thing should've died long ago. But Scott kept it running. The tractor had become a hodgepodge of random parts—a gray metal hood, red innards, and four different tires. Scott kept it spotless and rust-free, caring for it like it was part of their family. He was rocking out to "Iron Man," playing air guitar with a wrench and stomping to the heavy beat. Jason yelled for him, trying to push his voice over the tinny doom metal blasting from the boombox. When Jason's yells finally cut through, Scott ran over to us.

"Can you stand?" He lifted me off Jason's shoulders. I held his muscled arm, still feeling wobbly. When you're an eleven-year-old kid and blood is trickling down your face, it's scary shit. So I was relieved when Scott moved my hair out of the way, examined the gash, and said, "You scared the hell out of me. But the blood makes it look worse than it is. You'll just need a few stitches. And I bet your bell got rung pretty good."

Scott went inside the house, with its chipped white paint and warped windowsills. He came back with a wet hand towel and gently cleaned my wound. Wiping blood off my face, he said, "There you go, buddy. Let's get you to your parents."

I climbed in their dated Silverado after Jason, holding the towel to my head and trying not to get blood on the woven seat covers. My dad, Dan, was at work, so it was just my mom, Carrie, at home. An English teacher at Suffield Middle, she'd been on break for less than a week. I'm sure seeing her mangled son and his best friend, who was still wearing the blood-splotched white shirt, walk into the house was not a relaxing way to begin the summer.

"You weren't wearing your helmet, were you?" she said.

Scott followed us inside. "It will just be a small stitch job, Carrie," he said.

Mom examined my wound herself. "I could just murder you—and that includes you, Jason." She grabbed her keys from the ceramic bowl on the counter and told me to get in the car.

"Can J come?" It felt important that he went with us, as if he could protect me.

"Whatever. Come on," she said, already walking out the door. She hauled ass to Saint Francis Hospital, driving faster than I'd ever seen her. "Seriously," she said, "how many times do I have to tell you to wear your helmet? You only get one brain."

The worst part of the hospital visit was getting the shot of anesthesia in my dome. I almost yelped when the doctor unsheathed the needle. The shot stung intensely. After that, the fifteen staples felt more awkward and uncomfortable from the pressure than anything else. Mom looked away, but Jason watched with wide-eyed fascination as the doctor stapled my head shut. The official diagnosis: I'd suffered a mild concussion, plus the gash in my head.

I thought my split head might elicit some sympathy from my dad, but I was wrong. "Did I not tell you this would happen with that BMX shit?" he said after looking at my staples when we got home. He was already in a nasty mood because of a tough day at work. He went outside to change the oil in his truck, slamming the back door. The plastic blinds rattled against the window.

2

Things had been tense between me and my dad in recent months. In his prime, Dad was one of the best high school basketball players in Connecticut. College recruiters started going to his games and sweet-talking him when he was a sophomore. He hung up old clippings in our living room from the local paper that unironically said things like, "Dan Thompson is on his way to the top!" But he tore his ACL at the beginning of his senior year and was never able to play at the same level again. He always said he would've made it to the NBA if he hadn't blown out his knee. Who knows. Maybe he really would have. Either way, I felt like he tried to force that dream onto me, a lead blanket weighted down by his personal disappointment.

I'd been playing basketball with him since I was a little kid. If it was warm outside, we'd spend hours playing H-O-R-S-E and practicing fundamentals at a nearby elementary school. He showed me tapes of Larry Bird and Julius Irving, breaking down the mechanics of their movements. For a long time, I liked playing basketball with Dad—until, that is, he bought a whistle and stopwatch and started setting up little orange cones and making me run drills on the court. He began reading about unwavering sports dads like Earl Woods and Marv Marinovich and decided we needed to get serious early if I was going to be an elite player. Looking back, I don't think the strain and alienation in those father-son relationships was something he considered. With his bulky frame and thick neck, Dad seemed immovable, a man made of granite rather than flesh and bone.

He had coached all the youth teams I was on, but the gym teacher was the coach of the middle school basketball team. Dad was known among the local parents for being tough on me, and it got worse in sixth grade. High school was right around the corner, he said time and again, which was a time in a player's life that could make or break their career. During our last game before the playoffs, I zoned out in the fourth quarter and missed an easy pass. As the ball bounced out of bounds, Dad yelled from the stands, "Are you kidding me, Ry? Get your head out of your ass. You look like the fucking Rain Man out there." It was absurd, like something from a Will Ferrell skit—except this wasn't on TV.

I could feel my face redden. The gym got quiet, as if someone had let the air out of the room. Another kid's dad said, "Take it easy, Danny." Dad glared at him for a moment but then came out of it, realizing he was being an asshole—and people were watching.

I went on a scoring run after Dad's blowout. He cheered me on, too enthusiastically. It was his ham-fisted way of apologizing. Luckily for him, Mom wasn't there. They'd already been fighting about him being too hard on me.

"He needs to toughen up, Carrie," I overheard him say multiple nights when they thought I was asleep.

"Are you serious? He's eleven. Just let him have fun."

My dad also had a genuine tenderness to him. He, Mom, and I used to eat Ben & Jerry's after dinner and watch *Home Improvement* and *Step by Step*, two of Dad's favorite shows. He loved the predictability of those cheesy sitcoms. I'd lay against him, using his belly fat as a pillow. If I fell asleep, he'd wait until the show was over, then say, "Time to wake up, Ry Guy." I loved that: Ry Guy. But

Dad kept this part of himself hidden in public, and as I got older, it rarely surfaced at home.

∿

A month after my sixth-grade basketball season had finished, I was sitting at the dining room table staring out the window (not doing my math homework) when I noticed a big U-Haul pull up to the old farmhouse that sat beyond the woods behind our property.

Mom and I watched two parents and a kid who looked to be my age get out of the truck and start unpacking as a light rain started to fall. "I didn't know anyone was moving into the old Abbott place," Mom said. She decided to make them some snickerdoodles as a welcome gift, and she, Dad, and I went over the next night to drop them off.

The farmhouse was a bit run-down on the outside: it needed a new paint job and some other cosmetic work. With its sunken roof and weathered exterior, the barn seemed on the verge of collapse. The difference of my family's station in life was obvious. My dad owned a successful steel fabrication company that he'd inherited from his father. We would've been comfortable on his salary alone, but Mom never wanted to quit teaching. Dad and Grandpa had built our large ranch-style house, with occasional help from their carpenter friends, when Grandpa was still healthy. Not long after Grandpa died, Dad built a shop on the edge of our property. He kept it all in pristine condition.

Jason's mom opened their door after I knocked. She had short brown hair, glasses, and a rich, cigarette-tinged voice. "Oh my God, that's so sweet," she said as Mom handed her the Tupperware full of cookies. She told us her name was Laurie. "Scott, Jason, get in here," she hollered over her shoulder. "Our new neighbors are here."

Jason and Scott shuffled in from the living room and stood beside some boxes that had yet to be unpacked. Jason had piercing green eyes and a hawkish nose, and his black hair was cut into a bowl cut. He wore baggy cargo jeans, scuffed Airwalks, and a Korn T-shirt—a band my parents wouldn't let me listen to. After his dad nudged him, Jason introduced himself to us, shaking our hands and dutifully saying, "Nice to meet you." Scott, with his raggedy long hair and thick handlebar mustache, did the same.

They'd moved up to Connecticut from Arkansas, Scott told us, after his uncle died and left them the tobacco farm. "I was getting sick of working down in the coal mines," he said, "so I figured, what the hell? I always did love this place."

"I knew your uncle," my dad said. "Great guy." Born and raised in Suffield, Dad knew pretty much everyone in town.

While our parents talked, Jason asked if I wanted to check out his new bike. "Me and my dad just finished putting it together."

He took me back to his room. Band posters and pictures of BMX riders cut out from magazines were plastered all over the artificial wood walls. A bright red full-face helmet, covered in stickers and marked with scratches, sat on a shelf above his dresser. But the obvious centerpiece was the jet-black S&M[2] propped against his closet door. My parents had bought me a black Diamondback Viper, a decent general market bike, a few years earlier. At the time, I thought it was awesome—but, looking at Jason's bike, mine suddenly seemed corny. The S&M shield on the frame seemed so gnarly, especially compared to the neon pink Diamondback logo on my bike, which looked like it had been crafted and board-approved by some marketing agency in the eighties. I didn't know S&M was a rider-owned company, and I wouldn't have known then why that

_____

2 It's not what you're thinking. S&M stands for Scott and Moeller, the last names of the guys who started the company. That said, I'm sure they thought it was hilarious to have kids walking around schools across the country wearing S&M shirts.

was cool. There was just something about the shield, about the chunky red lettering on top of the yellow and white background—something that cut through like a bullet of truth.

As I gawked at his bike, Jason asked if I had ever raced. I told him that I'd messed around with wheelies and jumping off bumps in the road, but not much else. "I guess there's a good track in Hartford," Jason said. "And there's a race coming up. I read about it in *BMX Plus!*"

He reached under his mattress and pulled out the magazine. I was immediately captivated by its cover. In his red Schwinn jersey and blue sparkle helmet, Brian Foster (a.k.a. Blue Falcon) charged ahead of a pack of other riders, darting over a tabletop. With their full-face helmets and number plates, the racers seemed like a dystopian corps charging into battle. Before I could start looking through, though, my dad shouted, "Let's get going, Ry. It's a school day tomorrow."

"Can I borrow this?" I asked.

"Go for it," Jason said with a shrug. "I got the new one yesterday."

Back home, I pored through the magazine. Ramps, street, trails, racing—it all looked incredibly badass. With their tattered clothes and unkempt hair, the freestyle riders reminded me more of musicians than athletes. There were no coaches or parents. The riders seemed totally free. I saw the ad in the back pages for the upcoming race in Hartford that Jason had mentioned. I was too intimidated to try racing right away, but, when we were watching TV later in the week, I asked my parents to take me, just to watch.

"You want to go watch people ride their bikes in a circle?" Dad asked.

Mom answered before I had a chance. "Just because you don't get it doesn't mean it's stupid."

Dad looked at her like she'd slapped him. My mom was only five four, but, as far as I could tell, she was never scared of him, at least not outwardly. It took me years to understand why she fell for Dad in the first place. Her parents were beatnik painters from San Francisco who, inspired by Thoreau and Emerson, moved to Connecticut for a quiet, meditative life. Their approach to child rearing was to impose few rules and let my mom figure things out for herself. To her, their parenting came across more as laziness and narcissism than progressive open-mindedness. They also smoked a lot of weed. When she met my dad in high school, his discipline and steadfastness, not to mention his wavy hair and ripped arms, were highly attractive to her, even though she never thought she'd fall for a jock. But by the time I was in middle school, the stability she once saw in Dad had begun to look more like obstinance.

Mom looked at me and said, "I'll take you, Ry."

"Go ahead," Dad said. "I'm not stopping you."

The race was at the Hartford fairgrounds, in one of the corrugated steel buildings used for 4-H and rodeos. Walking through the doors, I felt like I was entering a new world. There were just as many adults as kids cruising around in jerseys and race pants. Their bikes were immaculate and highly specialized, seemingly capable of breaking the sound barrier. "Enter Sandman" blasted from the overhead speakers. People fixed their bikes next to the bleachers, behind which was a row of booths hocking bike parts, clothing, and safety gear you wouldn't find in most bike shops. The air pulsed with an independent, DIY spirit I'd never found in basketball. Each rider had placed stickers on their bike and helmet in their own personalized way. There was so much variation in the bikes themselves, from brand and make to color and components. Some riders wore cleat-like shoes that clipped to their pedals, while others wore skate shoes like Vans or Airwalks. I saw it right away: BMX could be an escape from my dad.

Mom bought us a bag of popcorn to share, and then she spotted the Abbotts in the aluminum bleachers. "Oh cool!" she said. "It's our neighbors." We wormed our way through people, who, with their leather jackets, bandanas, faded tattoos, and frizzy hair, looked like they were headed to a motorcycle rally. His helmet resting on his knee, Jason scarfed down a hot dog. His hair was matted down with sweat. A staticky voice came from the overhead speakers, calling the eleven-to-twelve-year-old Intermediates to the gate. In my eyes, Jason became a futuristic warrior when he got his bike and donned his full-face.

He and seven other riders balanced in their respective slots, their front tires pressed against the grated metal gate. Then a robotic voice came from the PA speakers: "Riders ready? Watch the gate." The gate slammed down in time with the last of three electronic beeps. I couldn't believe how quickly Jason and the other riders rocketed over the rollers and tabletops. It looked surreal, like their bikes were powered by invisible motors. Everyone on the track was fast, but it was obvious that Jason had something special. He not only won all his races that day, but he did it with seeming ease. He and his bike moved as one, gliding through the rhythm sections. He pumped to glean momentum from every possible source. Scott and Laurie cheered him on until their voices were hoarse. I wanted nothing more than to be out there with him.

Scott's huge grin poked out from beneath his prominent mustache when Jason came back over. "Did you have fun out there, buddy?" It was a common question, but I was surprised by it. My dad had never asked me that after a basketball game.

The next day, I woke up early, grabbed a shovel from Dad's shop, and started building a set of rollers on the dirt path snaking from my parents' property to the woods. I was almost finished with the first one when Dad came out of the house in his gray sweats and Celtics hoodie, tossing a basketball from hand to hand. "Let's get a practice in, Ry."

I kept packing the roller, slapping the dirt with the back of the shovel. "I'm going to ride out here today instead," I said, not wanting to look up at him.

"You don't want to get rusty, though. The season will be here sooner than you think."

"...Can't I just do this today?"

He clenched his jaw and gripped the ball with both hands. His mood could switch on a dime, and you never knew for sure what would set him off. Dad wasn't violent with me, aside from that time with the belt when I was in preschool, which very nearly pushed Mom to divorce him; but an incensed energy often coursed through his body and vibrated in the air around him, like it did now. Grandpa used his fists to teach my dad and uncle lessons. Dad and Uncle Billy endured some particularly brutal beatings when Grandpa drank, which was often. That violence was stored in my dad's body. If my mom wasn't part of the picture, I'm sure he would've unleashed it on me. There were many times just like this one, times when my dad fought hard to suppress his impulse to exercise control through pain.

He breathed exasperatedly and said, "BMX is a joke, kids' stuff. I know it seems far off now, but we need to stay dedicated if you want to play pro ball."

"I think I might be getting sick of basketball," I said almost without meaning to, feeling the weight of my words when I nervously met his stare.

Something short-circuited behind his eyes. "Fine. Go ahead and play in the dirt." He looked at me for a moment, spat on the ground, then walked off.

I picked up my bike and rode over the foot-high roller to pack it. I spent the rest of the day finishing it and building a second one, only going inside for lunch. Once the rollers were done, I tried manualing between them like I'd seen people do at the races. Not knowing how to leverage my weight, I wasn't able to keep my front wheel up. It slammed onto the top of the second roller, and I almost ate shit. I tried jumping them instead, which was surprisingly easier. In the air and right after I landed, my chest hummed. I had an immediate urge to recreate that feeling.

So I did.

Next thing I knew, the sun was setting, and a chill had suffused the spring air. Lying in bed that night, I couldn't wait to go back and ride my little roller section. I also dreaded fighting with my dad about it. The next time I told him I wanted to ride behind the house instead of going to the basketball court, he reacted with the same charged irritation.

"Life is work, Ry. You can't just quit when something gets tough." He'd just changed from his grimy work coveralls into the gray sweatshirt and sweatpants he wore when we practiced.

"Ease up on him," Mom said from the other room. "Do what you want to, Ry."

I wanted to laugh at Dad's deflated face but didn't. He watched me put on my shoes and hoody and go outside, knowing he couldn't say or do anything to stop me, not unless he was willing to stand up to Mom.

I came back inside later that evening to find Dad in the living room, watching an old tape of a Celtics vs. Bulls game when Larry Bird sank a game-winning jumper with Michael Jordan guarding him. We'd watched that shot together countless times. Dad had used the footage to show me what a proper fadeaway looks like, which, he said, was a timeless shot, both because of how effective and beautiful it could be. He patted the cushion next to him and said, "Take a seat, Ry Guy."

Even though I knew exactly how the game was going to end, I got caught up in the moment along with Dad as the Bulls pulled ahead of the Celtics in the final seconds. He got up as if the game were live, standing a few feet from the TV. When Bird hit the jumper and the stadium went berserk, Dad turned to me. "Can you imagine how good that felt? Look at that smile on his face. He's on top of the world." He sat back down on the couch and tousled my hair. His hand was huge. He could easily palm my head. "I always thought your jumper looked like Bird's."

3

I had made plans with Jason to meet at my house on Saturday and go ride. But earlier that morning, Dad caught me off-guard when he came to my room and asked if I wanted to play basketball with him at Suffield Park. He liked to go there when the weather was warm so we could have the full court to play. The hoop at our house was on a dirt and gravel driveway—not ideal for practicing in my dad's eyes. I was sitting cross-legged on the floor in my bedroom, rereading the issue of *BMX Plus!* I'd borrowed from Jason when Dad came to the doorway. "We can just play H-O-R-S-E and shoot around," he said, looking at me sheepishly.

"Um...okay." I couldn't bring myself to say no to him again. He looked desperate as he waited for my answer, and I didn't want to get into another fight. I figured if we left now, I could get back home in time to meet Jason.

On our way to the park, Boston's "More Than a Feeling" came on the radio. Dad turned it up loud, then blew into his Thermos of coffee and took a sip. "Your mom and I used to make out to this," he said with a little smile. Knowing it was a surefire way to make me laugh, he belted out the chorus like a cheeseball.

At the court, I shot some free throws and layups, which was how we always warmed up, and then I began shooting jumpers from different spots. I made three swishes in a row. The chain-link net sounded more musical than windchimes. "Gorgeous, Ry," Dad said after I sunk the third one. "Now let's see who's the horse's ass." It was the same joke he made every time we played H-O-R-S-E. He sent me a quick bounce pass, stinging my fingers a bit. "Ladies first."

There was a time when my dad would let me win, but those days were long gone. I'd never beaten him when he played seriously. One of his few weaknesses was hook shots, so I took a chance and tried one. I usually missed them, but the ball bounced off the backboard and through the net.

"Lucky shot, smartass." He was trying to keep the mood light, but he still got irritated when he missed. I could see it on his face.

I found a spot behind the hoop and arced the ball over the backboard. To my surprise, it also went in.

"Bullshit," Dad said. "I didn't realize we were playing clown ball." He got in the same spot and lined up his shot. He had the right arc, but he gave it too much power. The ball missed the rim entirely. I almost laughed but knew I should hold it in.

I jogged over to get the ball, then dribbled back to the free-throw line.

Dad said, "No more joke shit."

I shouldn't have done it: After acting like I was going to shoot a regular free throw, I turned around at the last second and bounced the ball through my legs. My reverse bounce shot barely brushed the bottom of the net, pretty much an air ball.

"Damnit." Dad snatched the ball. "Quit fucking around." He picked a spot in the bottom-left corner, then turned his back to the hoop as if someone was guarding him. He dribbled, made a quick fake, and spun around to send a picture-perfect fadeaway zipping through the net.

I went to the same place and was about to try a regular forward shot. Dad said, "You know the rules. Has to be exactly the same, or it's a letter." I thought about just going with the forward shot anyway. Instead, I turned around, faked, then shot the fadeaway. It bricked.

"Atta girl." Dad grabbed the ball and trotted to the other corner. He dribbled a few times and sank a three. Another perfect shot.

"I thought we were just having fun."

"What kind of pussy attitude is that?"

I tried the shot, but it hit the rim and bounced to the other side of the court. I didn't care about missing, not really. I was pissed that my dad always had to be such a hard-ass.

"Don't get your panties in a knot," he said before trying to hit a jumper from the top of the key. He missed, which surprised us both.

I got the ball and went behind the hoop again to shoot one over the backboard.

"You think I'm kidding, Ry? No more joke shit."

I looked at him and sent the ball into the air. I couldn't believe it: a swish. Dad looked like I'd punched him in the face.

"This is what you want to do? Just fuck around and never take anything seriously?"

"This is why I hate playing with you. You get on my ass about everything and take out all the fun. I'm done with basketball." Before he could respond, I said, "I'm just going to walk home."

He glared at me as if daring me to do it—so I left, slamming the gate to the court on my way out. Thinking about getting home in time to meet Jason and go riding, I started running as fast as I could.

Dad got in his truck and came after me. Driving next to the sidewalk, he barked, "Get in the goddamn truck!" Then, trying to contain his anger, "We can go home. I'll take you home."

I kept running, staring straight ahead.

"Fine, have your hissy fit." Dad sped off, engine roaring.

Suffield Park was three miles from our house, but I didn't need to stop because there was so much adrenaline pumping through me. By the time I got home, Dad was already in the kitchen drinking a glass of water, trying to cool down.

"What happened?" my mom asked me.

"Nothing," I said, out of breath. "I just wanted to run home."

She looked at me skeptically, knowing full well how much Dad and I had been clashing lately. Instead of prying, she changed the subject. "Jason came by looking for you about twenty minutes ago."

Anger flooded my body because I'd missed him. I hurriedly put on my jeans and went into the garage to get my bike, hoping Jason would be at his house. Hurrying past my dad on the way out, I could feel his eyes on me. I ignored him. I pedaled as hard as I could through the woods and then the Abbotts' tobacco field.

Laurie answered the door. "Yeah, Jason's here," she said. "Everything okay?" She must've seen how out of breath I was.

"I was just worried he'd be gone."

She went to the back of the house. I heard her say, "Ryan's here for you."

Jason came out with his bike, which gleamed in the sunlight. "This is your bike?" he asked, looking at my Diamondback like it was a turd. "You're going to fuck this thing up fast." He chuckled and said, "I thought you guys were rich."

Eager to show him up, I pedaled past him and into the woods.

4

Jason told me about another race in Hartford. I memorized the date and started practicing every day leading up to it. While eating dinner a few weeks after building my rollers, I asked my parents if I could try racing myself. I knew better than to ask Dad when we were alone. Before he had a chance to answer, Mom said, "You can give it a whirl. But we'll have to get you a good helmet." She looked at Dad, silently daring him to argue.

As usual, they'd been fighting at night in hushed tones that steadily grew in volume. I thought it was my fault. They often argued about politics—about the women who were coming forward to expose President Clinton's predatory nature (according to Mom, they were brave; to Dad, they were trying to get money) and about Dad regurgitating Rush Limbaugh's rants about "feminazis." In my head, though, my dwindling interest in basketball was the real center around which my parents' strife revolved. But even that didn't lessen the gravity pulling me toward BMX.

Dad was quiet, looking at the table. Then he said, "You're going to crack your skull. Just watch."

Back inside the metal building at the fairgrounds, I felt electrified all over again—this time more so because I was going to ride. We found the Abbotts and sat with them. Mom had bought me a bright yellow full-face helmet. I put it on when the announcer called for riders in the eleven- to twelve-year-old Novice class to start warming up. Jason raced in the Intermediate class already. He got up with me to take a few practice laps anyway.

I was terrified the first time I pedaled through the track. People sped past me on both sides like I was an idling Buick in the middle of the freeway. I thought someone was going to plow me over. I came in dead last in my first race, but I was in love. For one full minute, there was nothing but me, my bike, the track, and the kids charging past me. I didn't even hear the crowd. I was able to fully enter the moment, which never happened when I played basketball.

∿

Just as Jason had predicted, my Diamondback got worked: bent cranks, a broken headset cup, and a tweaked back end. Then, after the wreck where I busted my head open, I noticed that a weld on my frame had cracked. For my twelfth birthday, I asked my mom for a new bike (when Dad wasn't around, of course). She bought me a brand-new Schwinn, wheeling it out from the garage and into the living room after I opened my other presents. The bike's yellow frame and chrome handlebars glimmered. My dad was still pissed about me getting a concussion. Needless to say, my new bike did nothing to diffuse the tension in our house. It stressed me out when my parents fought, but my excitement at having a legit bike easily outweighed that anxiety.

I put on my helmet, which Mom made me promise to wear all the time after my crash, and rode into the woods, where I ditched it as soon as I was out of sight. Unless I was in a race, I didn't like wearing a helmet. None of the freestyle riders I saw in magazines wore them, and I knew Jason would make fun of me for having it on.

"This is a badass bike," Jason said when I got to his house. He examined the cranks and rotated the pedals backward to test the freewheel. We both knew it wasn't as cool as his S&M—Schwinn

was a corporate brand, not a core company—but it was undeniably a solid bike.

Scott came out of the house holding a can of soda. "You got a new ride, Ry? Let me see that thing." Despite having known the Abbotts for less than half a year, I felt completely at home with them. Scott looked over my bike, picking it up to check its weight and squeezing the brake lever. "This thing's light as a feather," he said. "You better watch out, J. Ry might start beating you soon." He took a swig of Dr. Pepper and quickly cleaned his mustache with his bottom lip. "Well, what the hell are you boys standing around here for? Go test that beast out," Scott said, motioning to the woods.

It wasn't long before I was riding along with the Abbotts to races across Connecticut, New York, and Rhode Island. With Jason and Scott helping me, I progressed quickly and accumulated enough points to get bumped up into the Intermediate class. I was a fast learner and practiced constantly between races, even though I felt like I was tiptoeing through a minefield every time I left the house while Dad was home. Try as I might, I could never beat Jason. He had something I didn't, and I couldn't quite put my finger on what it was.

Me (#24) chasing Jason (#17)

When school started and sign-ups for basketball opened, I knew I'd have to tell my dad all over again that I wanted to quit. That day in Suffield Park with him was my last straw, but I don't think he took me seriously when I told him I was done. He hoped it was just something I said when I was mad. For weeks leading up to what would've been my second middle school season, I'd been thinking about what I would say, the words ping-ponging in my brain. Finally, at dinner one night, I got up the nerve to tell him. I swallowed a bite of the Hamburger Helper he'd made for us, then looked over at him. "I just want to ride, Dad. I haven't wanted to play basketball for a long time." I looked down at my hands, which were shaking, albeit slightly.

He took a drink of his milk and set the glass down a bit too hard. The muscles in his jaw tensed. "There's no future in BMX. No college will give you a scholarship for popping wheelies. Those guys are burn-out losers."

I shrugged and looked away, pushing around the peas on my plate with my fork. I expected him to erupt, but he seemed more defeated than angry. No doubt my mom had already been talking to him about me quitting basketball. "Let him follow his passion," she said.

"Fine." Dad took another bite of dinner. "Whatever."

He didn't make eye contact or talk to me for the rest of the night. I couldn't help but compare him to Scott and be envious of Jason for having a dad who was so cool and supportive. I still look back on the times I had with Scott as some of the best BMX experiences of my life.

5

Scott shot himself on a Tuesday. It was almost a year after my crash and just before Jason's thirteenth birthday.

What Scott had never told my family was that he inherited the farm's debt along with its land. Laurie landed an office job with the City of Suffield shortly after they moved, but they were still hemorrhaging money. With more and more farms in the area getting bought out by corporate heavyweights, it was an uphill battle for Scott to push their farm out of the red. Soon, the debt had gotten worse than even Laurie knew. The bank was threatening to foreclose. I'm still not sure how Scott kept it secret.

Jason was the one to find his dad in the barn when he came home from school on what must've seemed like a regular March day. It was snowing, one of the last times before the trees started to turn green again. Jason called his mom at the office. She called 911.

I heard the siren when the ambulance passed by our house, not thinking much of it until our phone rang a little while later, and Mom answered. "Oh God," she said when Laurie told her what had happened. She cried hard but quietly, the news wringing her body. I pressed pause on my PlayStation controller and asked her what was going on. "Scott shot himself," she said. Thinking back on it now, I appreciate that she told me what happened in straightforward language. There was no gloss on her words. I held the controller tightly. It suddenly seemed like a strange and useless plastic object.

Dad's immediate reaction was anger, which was really just a shroud over heartbreak. He and Scott had been hanging out on their own, drinking beers in the shop or working on Scott's tractor. "Only a coward would abandon his family like that," Dad said when he got home and found out what happened.

"You don't know what he was going through," Mom said. "You think you do, but no one does."

Dad dismissed her words with a wave of his hand. "There's no excuse. It's the coward's way out, plain and simple."

None of it seemed real to me. I couldn't believe someone I loved could be gone so quickly—and with no warning. Scott had taken Jason and me to a race in Albany only two weeks earlier. We packed in his three-seater Silverado after putting our bikes in the flatbed. My front wheel spun in the wind when we got on the freeway. Scott put an AC/DC tape in the deck and cranked the volume.

"If this doesn't get you boys pumped up," he shouted, "I don't know what to tell you." He played drums on the steering wheel along with the marching riff of "It's a Long Way to the Top." Jason and I laughed as Scott looked at us and played air guitar.

Jason got locked up in a berm with another kid during the finals that day. I'd gotten eliminated in the previous heat because of a weak start. I was sitting with Scott, eating nachos in the bleachers, when Jason got tangled up and flung off his bike. He picked himself up and brushed dirt off his jersey. He wasn't hurt, but he was frustrated about losing, so he didn't talk to us when he walked his bike over.

"Don't worry about it, buddy," Scott said, giving the top of his son's shoulders a squeeze. "There's always another race." To help us forget about our bruised little egos, he took us to Baskin-Robbins before driving back to Suffield.

∿

It's been over twenty years, and I still stop myself from imagining what Jason saw in the barn. He only talked about it with me a handful of times. The first was when we were both very drunk and a little stoned during a trip to NYC. He started sobbing, and all I could make out was, "His fucking brains were on the wall." That's not the type of thing you ask someone to tell you more about.

They didn't find any drugs or alcohol in Scott's system, which made it all the more brutal. He was suffering with those thoughts alone, with nothing to cushion his pain. The bank foreclosed on the farm two months after Scott killed himself. Laurie had just enough in savings to rent a shabby little house in town, over by the hardware store. The bank ended up selling the Abbotts' farm to a corporation called Coalition Incorporated.

I remember being struck by how many people showed up at Scott's funeral. There were some familiar faces, but I'd never seen most of these people. Many of them came up from Arkansas. They packed into the pews in front of a large picture of Scott that stood behind his ashes. He had an entire life of interactions and friendships that didn't include our family, and seeing this was gutting. I'd only seen Dad cry one other time, at Grandpa's funeral. Tears welled in his eyes as Laurie broke down, trying to read the eulogy she'd written for her husband.

Jason's face twisted into a scowl as he stared blankly ahead. It was the first time he scared me. When he looked at the fake stained-glass windows of the church, it was clear how badly he wanted to smash them.

6

Jason and I became inseparable. After Scott died, it went without saying that he was welcome anytime at our house and I at his. Mom and Dad treated him as their own. Dad grilled deer burgers for us when he knew Laurie was working late one night. I asked Jason if he wanted to stay. He said he didn't want to interrupt our family dinner.

Dad overheard and said, "Bullshit. You're part of this family."

Laurie's strength blows my mind to this day. She took on a part-time job doing the books for a mechanic in addition to her full-time job with the City of Suffield. There were lean times, but she busted her ass to keep a roof over their heads and make sure Jason wouldn't be one of the kids who got teased because his shoes and clothes had holes.

Laurie put on a strong face in public, but when I'd go over to their new place, she seemed numb, barely there. I'd say hi and give her a hug, and it was hard to tell if she even knew who I was. She and Jason lived off mac 'n' cheese and frozen pizza for quite a while. My mom routinely made casseroles for me to bring over. I helped Jason do the dishes and clean up when it got messy in their kitchen.

Their new place seemed so tiny compared to the house on the farm, although it wasn't actually that much smaller. It was off-putting to see Laurie's old white Datsun pickup in the driveway without Scott's Silverado parked next to it. She sold the truck to one of the guys who worked for my dad. The Abbotts had an old green couch in the living room, and the indent where Scott used to sit was still there, the seat cushion worn dark and smooth. Neither Jason nor Laurie sat in that spot, not for a long time.

Jason and I both found escape and solace on our bikes, so that's how we spent most of our time. At races, we had already been airing the jumps higher than you're supposed to if you wanted to cut time. We'd begun building and riding the first iteration of our jumps in the woods a year earlier. We turned the little roller section I'd made into an actual double and expanded from there. Whether at our jumps or on the track, there was an added edge to Jason's riding after Scott's death. He never said as much, but he harbored a lot of anger toward his dad. He funneled that aggression into riding.

When taking a break from building our own jumps, we started riding at some older guys' trails in town. Jason had found them randomly one day, just pedaling around. The guys were in high school. They had two eight packs in this small, circular clearing in a thicket of trees not far from Jason's house. The guys seemed to hover, beyond gravity for a split second in the space between each lip and landing. As a racer, you're supposed to stay as low to the ground as possible while still clearing the jumps, pulling up and snapping your back end forward, like a wasp's stinger. These three guys focused their energy on going *up* instead of simply *forward*, pushing their front wheels into each landing on their way down to trace an arc in the air instead of a straight line. Their feet shot off their pedals when they did no-footers, and they fully crossed their arms and cranked their front wheels past their frames when they did X-ups.

Two of the guys rode FBM frames. The other had a Metal Bikes build. I'd heard of the companies but hadn't seen the bikes in person. The riders wore backward caps and baggy jeans, not tight-fitting race uniforms, and they cussed like drunken sailors. Jason and I made it through both of their jump lines first try.

"Damn, you little dudes are pretty good," one guy said. He lit a cigarette and took a drag, trying to look cool.

"There's no way we would've hit these when we were your age," his buddy added.

I'm sure those guys could see it in our toothy grins: Jason and I might as well have taken off our number plates that day because the track couldn't contain us anymore. The final nail in the coffin was when one of those older guys let us borrow *Seek & Destroy* on VHS. That was unequivocally a before-and-after moment for us. It changed how we saw BMX, showing us that what we did could be both more artful and more destructive than we'd ever imagined.

Since real street riding was relatively new, Van Homan's section of burly grinds and gaps blew everyone away. That part was epic, especially with Metallica's "Battery" for the soundtrack. The crash section in the video was absolute savagery. Guys smashed their bodies and faces into dirt, concrete, and handrails, getting completely pummeled. There was also a lot of gnarly tomfoolery in *Seek & Destroy*, like a dude breaking a bottle over his own head; riders wrestling in a van and slamming each other face-first into the floorboard; a guy shooting a bottle rocket out of his mouth; and a rider ripping his friend's boxer shorts completely off while the dude struggled to get away.

Jason and I were transfixed by the trail footage, though. The jumps in the video were massive, sprawling across much larger distances than we'd seen. We were used to three or four jumps in a row. But here were riders navigating serpentine paths of eight jumps or more, the lines needling through dense trees. The most majestic trail spot in the video, we'd soon discover, was a place called Posh.

In *Seek & Destroy*, Chris Stauffer and Garrett Byrnes floated above jumps as if they'd harnessed some weird magic, letting their back ends drift to the side. Even if you didn't know anything about BMX, you could watch that footage and get a sense of the weightlessness they felt in the air. It's one of the purest forms of existence, one of the rare times when the world, along with all of its pain, vaporizes.

Applied to riders like Stauffer and Byrnes, I've always thought the word "trick" seemed off, even though that's the word people have always used. I don't know what else you would call it, except for each specific thing—whips, tabletops, X-ups, turndowns, and three-sixties. "Move" and "maneuver" are both cheesy as fuck, but I think movement fits, even though it's too pretentious to ever catch on, especially with riders. If someone had told us in the years to come that we were performing movements in the air, that this style of riding was distinct from the more robotic, stunt-like tricks you'd see from Dave Mirra, we would've known exactly what you were talking about—and we still would've laughed in your face. That's it, though: there were different movements, and, especially if you were good, everyone did them a bit differently, enough to where you could get a sense of who the person was from their riding.

We went to a few more races after we saw *Seek & Destroy*. But it was obvious that part of our lives was over. We lazily pedaled around the track to the tired soundtrack of screaming parents. Racing suddenly felt like the BMX equivalent of Metallica's *Black Album*: regimented, predictable, tightly controlled. Trails were *Ride the Lightning* and *Master of Puppets*: aggressive, intense, profound.

7

Scott had given Jason this old video called *Freestylin' USA!* that was filled with dudes with permed mullets hopping around on flat ground like their bikes were pogo sticks. After seeing that, I associated freestyle BMX with neon frames, goofy tricks, eighties synth music, and Southern California—until we saw *Seek & Destroy*, that is. The trails and riders in the video were almost entirely East Coast. I still think that's where the best trails have been built. You simply don't get that thick, nutrient-dense soil out west, except for Oregon and Washington—the sticky, clay-infused dirt that, once packed properly, becomes hard and smooth as concrete.

It only made sense for us to build our own trails. There were hardly any street spots in Suffield. There wasn't even a skatepark back then. But there were endless stretches of woods. The woods behind my parents' land that butted up against the tobacco field were the perfect place. Coalition Incorporated, the company that bought the Abbotts' acreage, demolished the farmhouse and barn. A large steel warehouse facility shot up seemingly overnight. Tobacco conglomerates were constantly looking for debt-sunken farms in the area they could buy for cheap. It definitely wasn't the first time I'd seen it happen. But Coalition never expanded the field and leveled our jumps like we expected them to.

A worn trail cut through our woods. Our first line started when we turned my rollers into one big jump and added two more

40

doubles after it, the last one putting you on the edge of the field Scott had poured so much of himself into. I had read an interview with one of the Posh builders who said it was bad luck not to name your jump lines. We named our first line Battery after the Metallica song we both loved—and that became the tradition: naming our lines after (old) Metallica songs.

Each spring birthed a new iteration of our trails. We kept adding jumps to Battery until it consumed almost every inch of the original path. The jumps also got bigger, soon becoming taller than us, with gaps twice that, at least. We were completely enclosed by a cocoon of leaves, vines, and bark. Working that soil was a way for us to stay connected to Scott, although neither of us said as much.

Stupid as it was, Dad still resented me for quitting basketball. If anything, Scott's death only strengthened my dad's desire for control—and made him more frustrated when he didn't have it. Most times, when Jason came over to ride in the woods, Dad said something like, "I don't get why you'd want to waste so much time digging and popping wheelies. Seems like a circle jerk." It might've made more sense to him if we were striving for something tangible like X Games gold. But we weren't. We wanted to become pros; mostly though, we wanted to ride with great beauty. We had no interest in learning the circus stunts that win big contests. It didn't help endear my dad to freestyle when he saw the scenes in *Seek & Destroy* where riders chugged whiskey, broke bottles, shot fireworks at each other, and lit random shit on fire. "It's a bunch of work with no payoff," he said. "Plus, those guys are all ass clowns." When Jason came over to ride and dig, Dad didn't stop us. But he'd been drinking more since Scott died, and I worried he'd go on a tear when he was shitfaced and wreck our jumps.

I tried explaining to my dad why we were drawn to trails and style riding, but I didn't have the language to articulate our connection to it—and he didn't have the patience to help me bridge that gap. To us, BMX was closer to art than sport, and that distinction became much more pronounced when we quit going to the track. Racing was akin to using sheet music. We were ready to create.

Since Jason and I had started out racing, we knew how to pump, and it wasn't too hard for us to figure out how to pop off the lip to create that look and feel of floating. You pushed down at the bottom and used that force to spring off the top. You might think a burly, muscular build would be the ideal body type for a rider; but if you knew how to make your bike cooperate with physics, you didn't need a whole lot of muscle mass. As with most of our favorite riders, Jason and I were both lanky, although I always had more thickness to my arms and upper body.

Jason was doing clicked turndowns by the end of our second summer in the woods. His X-ups were the best I'd seen, including in videos and magazines. His arms would cross like a contortionist's as his front wheel almost spun a full rotation before he snapped it back; meanwhile, his back end would drift to the side to add that extra hint of grace. When he did turndowns, he would hover for a second before slicing his back end to the right, cranking his upper body along with his handlebars. It was all achingly beautiful. He was always one of those riders who, once he saw someone do a trick, understood the proper sequence of tiny movements and angle calculations to make it happen. He would quickly move from there to make each one his own. They became Jason's X-ups and Jason's turndowns instead of tricks people had been doing since the birth of freestyle.

Jason cranking a picture-perfect turndown sometime during high school

X-ups were easy for me to learn, although it took a while until I could tweak them like Jason. Turndowns were harder. Jason roasted one off the third jump in Battery, he and his bike moving as one. I yelled, "Dick!" which was a better compliment than regular praise.

I decided to try one on the same jump. I walked my bike to the top of the path, said *Fuck it* to myself, and pumped through the first two jumps. Off the third, I whipped my back end to the right as hard as I could, muscling my front wheel past the frame. My tire buzzed my jeans.

"Fuck yeah!" Jason shouted.

But then, when I tried to snap my bike back, it refused. I got stuck in the turndown position, so when I landed, my bike was perpendicular to the landing. It was one of those crashes where you know exactly how you're about to get worked, but you can't do anything to stop it. My back wheel dug into the landing, sideways. I got pitched into a pile of loose dirt next to a tree.

"Oh shit!" Jason dropped his bike, ran over, and reached out his hand. "You okay?"

I spit out a chunk of dirt, feeling its grit in my teeth and on my tongue. Worry was written on Jason's face, the same expression as when I knocked myself out years earlier. Not hurt in any serious way, I started laughing. Jason's high-pitched giggle reverberated in the trees.

"Your brake lever got stuck in your pocket." He picked up my bike and held it up for me while I brushed off my shirt and jeans and looked at the cut on my arm. Blood trickled down my forearm, but the gash wasn't anything to worry about.

"You need to lean back more," Jason said. "And don't muscle it so hard."

He was right, as always. After a handful of less dramatic attempts, I, too, knew that locked-in feeling of doing perfect turndowns, the feeling of getting purposefully tangled in your bike and merging with the metal. Even still, I was always two steps, at the very least, behind Jason. What mattered more was that, when we rode, we were able to disconnect from the things in life we couldn't control, or at least cordon them off to a place in our minds where they lost their sharpness.

8

Each winter became a period of mourning for our jumps. Standing in my parents' backyard, I could see enough of Battery to know how much the snow had eroded our work.

At the same time, that erosion pushed us to make the next iteration bigger and better. The summer after we learned turndowns, we got Battery running flawlessly, and then we started on Harvester. All winter, we'd been studying people's trails in videos and magazines, obsessing over the ways their lines connected and played on the natural flow of the land while we absentmindedly ate lunch at school. There was one month during our first year of high school when both our stores of magazines got confiscated, one by one, by various teachers, although I think most of them were relieved we weren't passing porn or bomb-building manuals back and forth during class.

When each new issue of *Ride* came out, we'd low-key quiz each other to make sure we were up on the latest news in the BMX world. For whatever reason, I was always better at retaining factoids than Jason. It drove him nuts.

"I can't believe Robbie Morales is thinking of ditching Terrible One to start his own company," Jason said, shoveling a chip through his cafeteria nachos to get an extra gob of meat. We sat at our own table, speaking in a language that was becoming increasingly

45

specialized. Our classmates didn't know what the fuck we were talking about.

"The article said he already left. He's starting a new company for sure." I took a sip from my Capri Sun, and then opened my Reese's and gave one to Jason.

"That doesn't sound right."

"Yeah, dude. The new company is called Fit." I pulled the magazine out of my backpack and showed Jason he was wrong.

Talking in a nasally nerd voice, he said, "Whatever, Encyclopedia Ryan."

In math class that afternoon, I noticed Jason staring off as if in a daydream. He thought about his dad constantly; it was obvious. During those moments, you could see something in his eyes get snuffed out, like a light getting turned off to reveal a dark window. I never knew what to say about it—about the void Scott left and the constant question of what things would be like if he were still here. I flicked a folded piece of paper at Jason to jolt him out of it. He flipped me off.

Scott's death had also yanked something from my guts. I knew my pain was nothing compared to Jason's—but it was still grief, raw and ravenous. When someone you're close to dies by their own hands, it leaves a specific kind of emptiness. It was so terrifyingly sudden, so crushingly permanent. One day, he was here, cheering Jason and me on at the track; the next, he was gone, a memory. The pain of losing someone to natural causes eventually finds resolve. I loved my grandpa, gruff as he was, but when he died from lung cancer, I found peace with it after a few months. I'd imagine Scott going to his gun safe and walking into the barn with the intention of ending his life—and it felt so wrong, like it was never supposed to happen that way. As abrasive and domineering as my dad could be, I was thankful he was alive. I didn't want to go through life without him. But there was no way I would talk to Jason about any of this. It made more sense to focus on digging and riding—things we understood and knew how to discuss.

By the time the weather had warmed up enough so we could go to the trails and not get our feet stuck in gluey muck, we had a defined idea of what Harvester would be. We had to get Battery running before we started, though. Our lips and landings got steeper every year as the trees blossomed with new life, emitting their virile odor. We used round-point shovels for digging and flatheads for packing. I'd "borrowed" Dad's nice wheelbarrow from his shop without him noticing. (I'd never seen him use it, anyway.) There was a patch of clay-heavy dirt near the top of the main path. We used that soil for the outer layer of each jump because it packed harder.

Building jumps was an art form to us, and we loved it, but you had to remind yourself of the release of pumping, flowing, doing whips, and following each other so closely between sets that your tires nearly touched. Winter used to bum me out to no end. I'm sure I whined about it and became a sulky little dick at home. Jason would get bored, too, but he weathered it better than me and even seemed to embrace the fact that summer wouldn't be as sweet without the winter doldrums. I'd say something at my locker like, "Fuck, winter is so much bullshit." And he'd say, "It's not that bad, Ry."

During the summer, I didn't mind the controlled, small-town vibe of Suffield—how, if you grew up there, you always saw someone you knew at the grocery store. Dad loved when people in Highland Market would say, "Hey, Danny Boy!" which had been his nickname since he was a kid. He loved knowing someone pretty much everywhere we went. When I first watched *Gilmore Girls*, the town in the show reminded me exactly of Suffield: a small, tightly knit (mostly white) New England community with its little cast of predictable characters. For the most part, the buildings, houses, and lawns in Suffield were well-kept. Ordered. It's a place where you could easily forget that New York, with its gritty complexity, was only two-and-a-half hours away. During the winter, heavy snow covered everything, pressing in. That's when Suffield felt claustrophobic. The town didn't bother me so much when the snow melted because there was so much freedom in our woods.

Jason and I studied every photo and clip of Posh in Bethlehem, Pennsylvania, to the point where we could draw the lines from memory. At Posh, they integrated more rollers before and between jumps, and the rhythm ditches were deeper than ours. Jay Lonergan, Magilla, and Devin Cole made it all look so pristine, plus the gaps were monstrous. Posh looked like a secret pocket of Middle Earth, the paths rising up and down and snaking in and out of each other like some hybrid between a pagan maze and an M. C. Escher drawing.

Although we didn't have as much space as Posh, we tried to harness a similar spirit with Harvester. We started the line with four rollers to create a gradual progression. Those led into one short-but-long double, which put you on course for two jumps, each bigger than the last, that shot you into a tight berm followed closely by three sizable doubles, each catapulting you toward the canopy of tree branches. At the end, you got launched off a big hip to put you on the path of the jump that butted up against the tobacco. When you surrendered to the rhythm of the jumps, you existed, for a brief but intoxicating moment, outside your body.

Suffield trails, 1999

I turned fifteen that summer. We had just finished our freshman year. It was this golden period—the last summer we didn't have any real responsibilities because our parents made us get jobs when we turned sixteen. We woke up early every day, ate breakfast, and headed to the trails. Jason would usually stay at my house since the jumps were so close. Our couch was his second bed. When we got on each other's nerves, we wrestled like brothers, putting each other in submission holds until, red-faced, one of us would tap out. It drove Jason up the wall when I tapped on his collarbone, so I made sure to do it as often as possible.

"Ry, seriously stop, I'll kill you," he said on a Friday night. His face turned red as I roughly tapped out Morse code gibberish on his bone. I was sitting on his chest. His legs flailed behind me. "You fuck, get off me."

The pleading stage was always the funniest—as long as you were the one on top. He found the base of our coffee table with his leg and used it for leverage to spring me off. When we got to our feet, Jason put his hands up like a boxer. I thought for a second he might actually swing.

Dad heard the ruckus from the bedroom and yelled, "Don't kill each other, you morons."

Jason and I looked at each other, and then doubled over laughing. We constantly pushed each other in every way we could, especially when it came to riding and building jumps.

Most people don't realize how much work it requires to build real trails. Think about it: two full lines of seven to eight jumps each—many of which, by the summer of 1999, were over five feet tall—with immaculately groomed paths, lips, and landings. Think about building those jumps by hand, one shovel-full at a time. Each line was its own story, and we wanted the story to have a natural flow. But it was difficult to get to that point. I doubt my hands will ever be as calloused as they were in high school. My calluses would swell up, looking like little mountain peaks. I'd cut them off with nail clippers only to watch them regenerate within a week. During dinner one night, Dad looked at my hands and said, "You wouldn't work that hard in the steel yard—and you'd actually *get paid* for it." But it didn't feel like work so much as fulfilling this deep sense of purpose.

"If you guys put that much work into school," Mom said, "you'd both get into Ivy League colleges." While she supported our riding, she wished Jason and I got better grades.

There was a clip in *Seek & Destroy* of these trail guys surrounding and then punching some kid on a mountain bike for showing up where he wasn't welcome. I never condoned that type of behavior, but I understood it. We put every fiber of our being into sculpting this dirt, into making sure each jump perfectly interwove with the next; so, the idea of random people showing up and fucking up our work made us want to kill someone. Imagine writing a novel as epic as *Moby Dick*, but one that people could somehow infiltrate and spoil. What would you do if someone debased your art? I'm glad Suffield was remote enough for no other riders to show up at our jumps uninvited. I remember this kid on a cruiser coming by one day. We stopped digging and stared at him. He never came back. The migrant workers Coalition hired to harvest tobacco would watch us occasionally. They'd shake their heads and laugh at us: two white boys playing in the dirt in which they toiled.

After Harvester came into being, we started laying tarps and upside-down strips of old carpet over the jumps to protect them from the snow, a tactic we'd picked up from an article about the trail scene in Rhode Island. Along with the wheelbarrow, I took a few tarps from Dad's shop without him noticing, and we picked up some rolls of old carpet from a metalhead carpet installer Jason's mom knew from AA. The guy had the rattiest mullet I'd ever seen.

We could ride each year until the snow stuck, usually near the end of October. There were a handful of times when, shooting hoops in our driveway, Dad asked Jason and me if we wanted to play a game of H-O-R-S-E with him. I felt bad seeing his deflated face when we told him we were going to ride, but our time in the woods was limited each year, and we needed to make the most of it.

During fall, I loved how the dry rustle of leaves mixed with the zip of our tires and the roar of our freewheels, how the woods blurred into a yellow and red and orange tapestry as you ripped through the jumps. But fall was also a death knell. I'd start to feel a weighted dread in my chest before I went to sleep. Our years were divided in half: trail riding and no trail riding. It felt right, covering our jumps every winter to protect them, almost like a burial ceremony.

9

Jason and I were hanging out in his room, poring over the new issue of *Ride*. It was early December, and Suffield was smothered in snow. We were restless. There was a feature in the magazine about Matt Beringer, an off-the-wall rider from Utah, and the bowl ramp he'd built in his two-car garage so he didn't lose his mind over the winter. In order for the setup to fit in such a small space, he made the transitions super steep. He painted a woozy, tripped-out American flag on the face of the ramps.

"It would be so sick to ride that with Beringer," I said.

"We should build a quarter pipe in your dad's shop," Jason said. "It's huge. We could build a full skatepark in there."

"He fucking hates BMX."

"Just ask him."

"You've never seen him when he gets fully pissed. It's scary."

Jason kept thumbing through the magazine. "Maybe my mom will let us build something in our garage."

The next day at school, he told me he'd talked Laurie into keeping her rusted truck in the driveway so we could build two small quarter pipes in their garage. "We just have to get the wood." He said it with a glint in his eye that told me he already had a plan. "There's a construction site near my house with a bunch of loose lumber. The crew won't be back until winter's over."

"My dad will beat my ass if we get caught. Probably yours, too."

"We won't. If we go by there with my mom's truck and just load it up in the morning—and act like we're supposed to be there—no one will fuck with us."

"…I don't know, J."

Against my better judgment, I went with him to the construction site at around ten on Saturday morning. Laurie would sometimes let Jason use her little truck, despite him only being fifteen, as long as he promised not to drive like an asshole. As dumb as the plan was, there was also some logic to it. If we tried to steal the wood in the middle of the night, one of the neighbors would know something was up. If we stole it during the day and acted casual, we might actually get away with it.

Driving up to the site, my heart beat out a double bass rhythm that would sound at home on a Slayer record. The sun reflected off the snow to create a blinding brightness. "Are you sure about this?"

"Just act normal, and we'll be good," Jason said.

He backed up to the section of the skeletal house-to-be where he knew the wood was stored. Without wasting any time, we got out and began stacking two-by-fours and sheets of plywood in the back of the Datsun. I started laughing and couldn't stop, which used to happen when I got nervous. Jason told me to shut the fuck up.

"What are you boys doing in there?" It was an elderly man wearing one of those old-school hunting caps with flaps over the ears. He'd walked up without us noticing.

I froze.

Without hesitating, Jason said, "We're just getting this wood for my mom's friend, Earl, so it doesn't get ruined in the snow."

"He's paying us to take it to his shop," I added, surprised at how easily the lie slipped out.

"Well, good on you," the guy said. "My bum of a grandson could use some of your initiative."

"Thank you, sir," Jason said, smirking. "You have a good day."

As the guy walked off, it took everything in me not to bust out laughing. Jason shut the door to the flatbed, and we drove off, giggling like maniacs.

Back at his house, Jason opened the garage door, and we stacked the lumber inside. Laurie poked her head in from the house. She was a certified rocker in the seventies and eighties. She had a weathered Led Zeppelin tattoo on her right shoulder. It was those weird little symbols for each member of the band, which I've always attributed to whatever weird wizard shit they were into. She'd quit smoking when she got pregnant with Jason, but her voice still sounded like she smoked a pack a day.

"Um, excuse me," she said. "Where'd you boys get this wood? It's brand-new."

"My dad had it in our shop to build a shed, but it's been sitting there forever, so he let us use it." I instantly felt guilty for lying to Laurie, who was essentially my second mom.

She looked at me, skeptical. "You know I love you, Ry. You'd be an asshole to lie to me."

"It's all good, Mom," Jason said, holding up two fingers like a smartass. "Scout's honor."

She didn't believe us, but she shook her head and went back inside anyway. Before closing the door, she turned and said, "If the cops come, I'm turning you in."

Jason's dad had an old circular saw, a drill, and some other tools they still kept. We'd both taken woodshop and had grown up with mechanically inclined fathers, so we knew some construction basics—just enough to be dangerous. We got started, cutting plywood and studs and piecing it all together. Jason went to his room to get his boombox, and we listened to Sabbath's *Master of Reality*, letting the disc play through multiple times.

It quickly became clear how tight our setup needed to be to fit in the garage. The transition of the first quarter pipe took up too much room, so we made the second one even steeper. Instead of properly measuring out the plywood so it would adhere to our shoddy frames in one piece, we drilled stray pieces into the divots. We finished both three-foot quarters by around nine that night. We pushed them against opposite walls, trying to keep them as far from each other as possible, but there was only three feet (or less) of flat ground between them.

You had to ride straight up one ramp and come onto the other backward before you could start turning around to do airs and stalls. You also had to get used to one ramp being steeper than the other. The quarter pipes slammed against the drywall every time we rode up them, seeming to shake the entire house. It took me longer than Jason, but I eventually got the hang of the ramps.

It suddenly didn't matter as much that Suffield was buried in snow.

"Oh God," Laurie said when she came back in to see our handiwork. "What have I let you do to my garage?" Jason and I laughed as she looked over our Frankenstein setup. "Well, let me at least see you ride it."

We both took a few runs, stalling on the lips and airing out as much as possible without hitting our heads on the roof.

"That slapping is going to drive me up the goddamn wall, and it feels like an earthquake inside the house. Can you at least call it for tonight?"

"For sure, Mom," Jason said.

When I told my parents about Laurie letting us build ramps in her garage, Dad said, "She's nuts to let you bring that shit into her house."

"It's not like she's giving them drugs," Mom said. She looked at me. "I think it sounds cool."

My dad had a way of looking at me that oozed disdain. He trained that look on me now. Another basketball season was in full swing, so he was especially irritable. I'd quit three years earlier, but he wouldn't let it go. His buddies were constantly bragging about their sons' sports achievements, so that didn't help. When they asked him what I was up to, the great Dan Thompson had to tell them his only son spent all his free time popping wheelies.

The look on Dad's face was a vacuum for my self-esteem—and it only strengthened my desire to be in the garage with Jason.

10

My mom took us to our first BMX night at the Incline Club skatepark in New Jersey near the end of January. It was a massive warehouse facility with every type of ramp you could imagine, not to mention that pros rode there all the time. When I asked her if she would, Dad overheard and said, "The fuck you want to go to Jersey for?" He turned off the TV, waiting for an answer. I didn't bother giving him one. Mom understood when I showed her a picture of the skatepark.

For her, taking me and Jason to New Jersey to ride was a way of needling Dad. As stressful as it was when they got into fights, part of me was almost relieved: it felt like they were finally being honest with each other. Truth is, Mom didn't seem to like Dad much anymore. I think Dad would've been willing to work things out, maybe even go to a marriage counselor, in spite of the fact that he hated therapy culture. But it's clear to me now that Mom had outgrown him. She never stopped learning, whether about different eras of literature, parts of the world, or classical music. Dad was the same guy she had met back in high school. Growing up, I felt that fissure more than I understood it. There were times when they seemed to remember why they had fallen in love—like when Dad came home with a box of Mike & Ike's because a) they were Mom's favorite candy, and b) she had gotten behind on grading, and he knew she'd want a sugar rush; or when Mom ordered pizza for everyone at Dad's warehouse at the end of a tough week. But those moments were few and far between. More often than not, life at our house was a domestic Cold War, with passive-aggressive comments and a routine chilliness between my parents.

My dad spent more time drinking in the shop as their marriage strained. He said he was working on his old Bronco, but it was obvious what he was up to. He'd stumble into the house after Mom and I had gone to bed, clomping down the hall with the agility of a toddler. The smell of beer seeping through skin lingered outside my door in the mornings.

I was excited to escape the tension in my home life for a night, not to mention ride a world-class indoor park. On the drive down to New Jersey, Mom asked if we'd been talking to any girls. Jason's face turned red, and he looked out the window.

"Not really," I said. "I feel like I don't have anything in common with any of them."

"Well, Einstein, you have to actually talk to them to find out." Fleetwood Mac's "The Chain" began playing on the radio. She turned up the stereo and said, "This song never gets old."

I looked at Jason and rolled my eyes. "This stuff is dad rock. Or I guess I should say mom rock."

As an answer, Mom turned the stereo up more, singing along with the lyrics about a relationship falling apart.

When we got to the Incline Club, Jason and I walked our bikes into the skatepark while Mom filled out our waivers at the front counter. She said she was Jason's mom to make the process easier.

We knew a lot of pros rode at Incline, especially during the winter. It was still a holy shit moment when we walked in and saw half of the Little Devil team on the deck of the mini ramp: Van Homan, Garrett Byrnes, Josh Stricker, and Pat Juliff, plus a few of the Pennsylvania trail riders we'd been obsessed with. That's one of the things I'll always cherish about BMX: access to the best in the world. Try getting a chance to meet LeBron James, Megan Rapinoe, Beyoncé, Brann Dailor, or anyone else who's known across the world for being the best at what they do. It won't happen. Riding BMX, you'd simply run into these people, especially on the East Coast during this time. Here were the guys we'd been studying in magazines and videos. They had that famous person glow. Those first few times we met pro riders, I remember becoming aware that any footage or pictures we saw of them were at least a few months old—so everything about them, from their tight T-shirts and shaggy hair to the way they carefully arranged stickers on their frames and helmets, seemed cutting edge and endlessly cool.

We didn't only get to watch our favorite riders from front-row seats. We were invited to participate, to test whether or not we were equipped for that level of riding. Although we were only fifteen, Jason and I knew we could hold our own. That didn't stop my hands from fluttering like butterfly wings as I jockeyed for position on top of one of the quarter pipes. Jason found an opening first and, without having spent much time riding box jumps or skateparks in general, he sprinted at the monolithic vert wall, glided to the top, pumped the transition coming down, and blasted the six-foot box jump, clicking the fuck out of a turndown. Garrett Byrnes and Van Homan both shouted, "Yo!"

Derek Adams, the owner of Little Devil, was there, too, riding and filming. Unbeknownst to us, he was filming for *Criminal Mischief*, the follow-up to *Seek & Destroy*. Since it came out, there's been a solid contingent of people who argue that *Criminal Mischief* is the best BMX video ever made. They're not wrong. So yeah, we were there for the clips of Garrett riding the spine, floating threes-sixties like Jordan dunking from the free-throw line; of Juliff doing the big quarter-to-quarter wall-ride gap both ways; and of Van ice picking that ten-plus-foot wall off the five-foot quarter while everyone in the park went nuts.

The thing about BMX was that you could see it in videos and pictures and still have very little conception of the speed and power you'd see in person—of how gnarly and huge it all was at the pro level. These guys rode with scorching intensity. When Van, Garrett, and Stricker did wall taps above the quarters, their back tires cut into the wood like hatchets.

While it was obviously mind-blowing to see some of our favorite pros ride, and it made us giddy when they asked us our names and where we were from, that night also made me realize once again how fucking good Jason was—and that I belonged here, too. Another thing about riding with people who were really good: it pushed you much harder than you would yourself. You felt a sudden imperative to go higher and faster. The boundaries you would've imposed if you were alone evaporated.

Jason and I both got clips that, to our absolute glee, showed up in the not-so-secret end section of *Criminal Mischief* when it came out a year later: Jason boosting an invert out of the mini ramp, turning his bike far enough upside down so his front tire grazed his shoulder, which I'd never seen him do before that night; and me cranking an X-up past two-seventy over the spine, airing it to the point where I felt a rush in my stomach as I nosedived back into the transition.

After the session, Derek Adams brought Jason and me out to his car and floated us a couple shirts. Street was becoming the focus for more and more riders, so he was psyched that we were legit trail rats. Jason got a black shirt with the classic LD logo with the little horns, and I got the 666ers mock basketball T-shirt in gray, which I knew my dad would hate; he loved both God and the 76ers. (He might've been the only Celtics fan in New England who was also a fan of the Sixers.)

"Your inverts look like Jason Enns's," Derek told Jason. I wouldn't have admitted it, but I wished he was as impressed with me.

Mom had been hanging out in the bleachers off to the side, cheering along when we were ripping but also being cool enough not to draw attention to herself. We came back inside with our new shirts and rode over to her. Then Jason decided he wanted to blast one more invert before we left. He'd been doing them all night, but now he was the only one out there. Time seemed to slow as he rocketed off the coping and turned his bike perfectly upside down, sucking his frame and bars into his body.

To Garrett Byrnes, Van Homan said, "That kid fucking rips." Jealousy singed my face, but I also felt proud of Jason. Him getting that kind of respect meant I would be on those guys' radar soon, too. When I told Jason what Van said on the way home, I thought he might swoon.

Mom took us to Incline again the following month, and the month after that. By the end of February, we had invitations to ride Posh in Bethlehem and the Little Devil ramps in Philly.

11

During an Incline session in late February, we met Devin Cole—one of the main Posh builders who also rode for FBM and Manmade—and some of his friends. Devin was a burly guy. He had shaggy blond hair, a large nose, and a short, reddish beard. He wore tight T-shirts even though his gut popped out, and he always seemed to be smirking. To us, Devin was the Ernest Hemingway of trail building. It was obviously rad to meet him, but I could tell right away he was one of those people who never turned off smart-ass mode. If you said something dumb, he'd immediately mock you. You always had to be on guard around him.

At the end of March, Devin invited Jason and me on a NYC trip with him and a few guys from Bethlehem. He asked Jason off-handedly at the end of a session, like it wasn't a big deal—but it was a thrilling moment for us. These guys were going to show us some street spots, and they had a place to stay. All we had to do was show up. Laurie had bought Jason a beater navy blue Cutlass for his sixteenth birthday. He'd been driving illegally since he was fifteen, so she wasn't worried about letting him drive a couple hours to New York—even though, technically, he was required to have an adult in the car. (Even my parents let me flout this rule when I got my license.) The night before we left, we stayed up late watching *Full Metal Jacket* because we were too excited to fall asleep. We woke up early, loaded our bikes on the rack of Jason's car (the back of the

Cutlass was covered, pretty much immediately, with scratches from our pedals) and drove down to the city.

We'd each been there multiple times, but our parents didn't like it much. How did Dad phrase it? Oh yeah, "Rat-infested shit hole." Mom thought it was too chaotic, and Laurie liked to see a show or concert there every once in a while, but that was it. It was ill-advised to let two teenage kids loose to stay with a bunch of older BMX dudes in New York City, but I eventually talked my mom into it, making it very clear that DEVIN COLE had invited us on the trip—and we'd be riding with ACTUAL PROS. Since Jason and I would be together, she thought we'd be fine. Aside from getting peeved at the partying and antics, I didn't think my dad paid much attention to my BMX videos, so I was surprised when he remembered that Devin rode for FBM, which stands for both Fat Bald Men and Fire Beer Mayhem. Each one was fitting, so I'm sure you can imagine what their videos were like.

"There's no way we're letting you stay with those degenerates," Dad said when Mom brought up the idea to him.

"I'm sure they just act like that for the camera," Mom said. "Right, Ry?"

"Yeah, for sure. Devin is a lot different in person. He's actually super mellow."

"I guess the decision's already made then," Dad said. "It's not like anyone in this family gives a shit what I think." He put on his steel-toes and walked outside to "work on the Bronco."

My parents had been fighting for what felt like a full month leading up to the weekend of our New York trip. Most of their arguments followed the same predictable pattern. Dad would say something about how environmentalists, feminists, and pretty much everyone else under the liberal umbrella were overly sensitive divas who had no idea how the world worked. Mom would counter and say how shortsighted and stubborn Republicans were, whether it was about gun control, global warming, or trickle-down economics. The argument would devolve into Dad saying Mom needed to get off her high horse and quit acting like a stuck-up...person (he always pulled his punch and didn't call her what he was obviously thinking), and Mom telling Dad he was a pig-headed chauvinist. When I think back on these arguments, the subtext seems so clear: Dad was asking Mom why she'd changed, and Mom was asking Dad why he'd stayed the same.

Pulling away from the house in the Cutlass, a weight lifted off my shoulders. Sometimes, I wanted to talk to Jason about my parents' strained relationship or how my dad had been getting wasted almost every night. But I always stopped myself. I didn't want to whine to someone who only had one parent.

Jason and I were bursting with giddiness as we roasted down I-95—all the trees on both sides of the road newly green—and blasted Glassjaw's *Everything You Ever Wanted to Know About Silence.* We were just getting into that type of hardcore, and we'd discovered the band, like so many others, in a BMX video. The breakdowns, weird rhythms, and mix between screams and effeminate melodic vocals felt so fresh, a new metallic style that had this raw, serrated emotion to it. I loved metal, but I was also getting tired of the macho façade you see with a lot of metal bands. I wanted aggression *and* vulnerability. The CD player was the first thing I remember Jason buying for the Cutlass, which leaked oil and smelled like burning plastic. He'd gotten a job working in the produce section of Highland Market, and he spent a full paycheck on it.

We were supposed to meet Devin at an old apartment building in Brooklyn, the directions for which I'd printed off MapQuest. As soon as we started to hit traffic, Jason's arms tensed, the veins on his neck popped out, and he became hyper-focused on driving, staying in the slow lane and making sure not to go over the speed limit. He was used to driving in Suffield, where traffic was nonexistent. He rarely showed fear, so I thought it was hilarious as he nervously looked in every mirror when someone honked. He was driving how he said never to ride: scared and tense. His nervousness eventually carried over and started making me feel on edge, too. When I saw a couple in a truck with matching mullets, I pointed them out, trying to get Jason to laugh. But he kept his eyes glued on the road. It was a relief when we got to the building and found a parking spot in front. Jason somehow parallel-parked the Cutlass perfectly.

Manhattan was so dense and crowded, I couldn't see how people actually lived there. Brooklyn was more mellow and spaced out. It still seemed gnarly, with trash strewn on the sidewalks and homeless people walking around, but I felt like I could breathe. Although I'd been to the city with my parents, it now seemed like a new frontier. Devin and his two friends came down from the brick tenement to meet us.

"If you guys got any bags or anything you don't want stolen, you should bring them up," Devin said when we got out. Aside from our bikes, Jason and I only had the clothes we were wearing. We told him we were good.

Devin was in his thirties at this point, and his two buddies, Trevor and Ben, were in their mid-twenties. There's a lot of mentorship in BMX, so the older-guys-hanging-out-with-teenage kids thing didn't seem that strange until I was in my early twenties myself. Trevor was one of those angle-hair guys. Slender with a symmetrical jaw and perfect teeth, he'd bleached the chopped edges of his brown hair. He was the first BMX dude I remember seeing who wore girl jeans, which became a huge trend not long after, largely because everyone wanted to look and ride like Mike Aitken.

Ben, who everyone called Neb for whatever reason, was harder to read, though I'd soon realize that the seeming thoughtlessness of his style—plain black T-shirts and slim-cut Wranglers—was highly intentional and specific, much like his riding. Neb's forehead looked too long for his face, and he had small, beady eyes.

We pedaled for a few blocks. Jason and I struggled to keep up as these guys darted in front of cars and dodged people on the sidewalk, all to a steady soundtrack of honking horns and people yelling at us.

We met up with some NYC locals—Tyrone Williams; Ruel Smith, who everyone called Wormz; Vic Ayala; and Edwin De La Rosa—all of whom were about to get national attention, especially Vic and Edwin. None of these guys had brakes, and it was about six or seven years before everyone started riding brakeless. They rode faster through the busy streets than Devin and his friends, narrowly dodging cars and laughing about it.

Street riding was obviously gnarly, but, to be honest, I saw it as a huck show: guys hurling themselves at huge rails and over ridiculous gaps and kind of hoping for the best. There didn't seem to be a whole lot of finesse to it. As Edwin, Vic, Tyrone, and Wormz wove through people and traffic, they bonked little side rails and curbs; grinded un-waxed ledges with steel pegs, sending that ripping screech echoing off buildings; and hopped on and off clanging storm doors like dirt jumps. It was the first time I saw the true beauty of street riding—saw how, in the right hands, an entire city could become a canvas, which was especially rad because none of these things were meant to be ridden. So it was all this radical shifting of meaning, purpose, and power. To this day, one of my favorite things is to watch good riders flow on their home turf, whatever that may be. Video parts and photos are sick, of course, but I've always thought this type of everyday riding is a truer window into a rider's skill.

After pedaling for what felt like a full hour, we cut through a maze of side streets and ended up at the Brooklyn Banks, one of the most iconic spots in the city. It's a long brick plaza under the Brooklyn Bridge with banks leading up to walls and multiple rails with perfect run-ups. It looked like a level from *Tony Hawk's Pro Skater*, like it was built for us. Intimately familiar with all the little imperfections and bumps of these brick embankments, Edwin blasted heavy technical tricks, making complex sequences look effortless. Tyrone was doing wall-rides above the flurry of tire marks and spinning off to land backwards, and Wormz did this gnarly vertical smith stall to one-eighty, chipping the concrete with his front peg. The sun had gone down, so it was getting chilly. Jason and I sat on our bikes, put on our hoods, and watched, blowing into our hands to keep them warm.

"Follow me on this wall-ride," Devin told us, coming up from behind. Having only done wall-rides at Incline, I followed Jason, hopping on and off more easily than I'd anticipated, immediately juiced by the feeling of slithering up a concrete wall. It didn't take Jason or me long to feel solid enough to sprint at it and pop off. Wormz said, "That trail style," when I boosted off the wall and glided back into the bank. With no callout or fanfare, Vic grinded the handrail that ran down the stairs adjacent to the banks, sending percussive notes back into the city.

The first Animal video came out a year later, showing the world how good these guys were. There were so many moments in our BMX life like this: when Jason and I were privy to its evolution—and, eventually, active participants in it, although that's much truer for him than me. Once you spent time in this world, you saw how small it was. Everyone knew everyone. But even then, I never took these moments for granted. I loved how they returned me to that joy and awe I had when I first discovered BMX.

A few homeless people were camped out on the other side of the plaza, where the banks were shorter. Devin and Trevor made their way over, which we realized when we heard Trevor's impish laugh. Jason, Neb, and I rode over to find Trevor stepping on a Snickers, smashing it into a pancake blob on the filthy concrete and saying to a homeless guy, "You only get the money if you eat the whole thing," to which the man said, "Yeah, that's fine."

I wish I could tell you that I didn't become one more laughing ghoul alongside Devin, Trevor, and Neb as we watched the man eat soiled candy for ten dollars—and I wish the same for Jason. The guy's jaw popped as he chewed. "Not bad," he said.

I wish I could say I didn't push past the sickly dread of watching another human get demeaned so I could laugh alongside some BMX riders I admired. It was far beyond a red flag moment. It was a cosmic billboard telling us to get the fuck away from these guys. But at that point in our lives, we wanted nothing more than to become part of their world.

∿

After the session wound down, Devin mentioned there was a party back at his friend's apartment. Edwin said they were going to keep riding instead. He pedaled off with Wormz, Tyrone, and Vic.

As obvious as it was that BMX fostered a hedonistic party culture, I still got a rock-in-the-stomach feeling of dread when I realized Devin, Trevor, and Neb were going to get drunk. A block away from the apartment, Devin stopped at a bodega and asked if we wanted anything. Jason and I looked at each other, and then back at Devin.

"Wait, have you guys ever drank before?"

I made up some story about stealing my dad's whiskey and drinking it at our trails, and Jason went along with it. It was obviously bullshit.

"Oh God," Devin said, laughing. "I'll get you guys a Mickey's to split. You can put orange juice in it so it doesn't taste like piss."

When we got up to the apartment, there were thirty or so people stuffed into this grimy two-bedroom (I never knew whose apartment it was), including a few additional members of the FBM team, as well as the thick-set, tattoo-covered company owner, Frank Williamson. It was a haze of smoke and bodies in there, Slayer pounding in the background. The Little Devil team had a reputation for being wild, but FBM took it all two steps further, showing guys blowing up old cars in videos alongside some of the most raw and stylish riding you could find. The frames and parts themselves were so goddamn well-made. When my dad looked over Jason's FBM frame a year later, he said, "Those dirtbags from your videos make these?" surprised to see such immaculate craftsmanship from the hands of men who rode kid-sized bikes and played with fire.

The thing about BMX parties: the culture of egging each other on and one-upmanship translated directly to drinking, and there were usually ten or more horny-as-fuck young men (and often teenagers) to every woman.

Jason and I didn't identify as straight edge, which was fairly widespread on the East Coast back then, but we did associate partying with the people at school who acted like the world began and ended in Suffield. My dad's drinking never made alcohol seem appealing, plus Jason's mom was a longtime AA member. She didn't get all D.A.R.E. on us, although I do remember her saying, "I wouldn't be alive if I hadn't quit the sauce when I did." We nodded like we understood what she was talking about.

But none of that mattered because when a well-known trail rider and builder[3] hands you and your best friend a forty after chugging the top off and pouring in some orange juice, chances are that you'll both drink it, at least as much as it takes to get wasted, which isn't much for two skinny teenagers. After that, it only makes sense that you'd both try to hit a sloppy, saliva-soaked blunt as Devin watches, laughs, and films. Given the previous sequence of events, it's no surprise when you find yourself laughing alongside the owner of FBM as he films his buddy pull down a girl's jeans and write "FBM" on her bare ass with a black marker. Considering all those things, it will seem inevitable to hear Trevor repeatedly ask/tell that same girl to fuck your (underage) best friend until Jason surprises everyone and tells him to leave her alone. By the time you find yourself in the bathroom, taking turns throwing up and listening to your closest friend sob and tell you about finding chunks of his dad's brain on the wall of his barn, it's almost a relief.

∿

The next morning, it took me at least ten minutes of staring at the smoke-grayed spackle ceiling to realize that it all actually happened. Jason's head was resting on my chest. I nudged him awake, and we got out of there. We drove through early-morning New York, its usual roar reduced to a gentle drone, without saying much beyond me reverse engineering the MapQuest directions and Jason periodically asking for clarification.

If I looked back on all this and said I wish we would've made the right decision afterward and stayed as far away from those guys as possible, it would be glossing over the fact that that night and everything after was already locked into place for us. Devin

---

3   In the years to come, Devin and his crew would become the go-to team for building dirt jumps at X Games and most other major contests. If you wanted your jumps built right, that's who you hired.

and his friends weren't some local high school heroes. They were nationally renowned riders. Our instinct to blend in with them swallowed everything else.

12

12

My lungs ballooned in my chest when one of the hot girls, Alissa,
walked up to me in the hall at school the following week and handed
me a note with my name, surrounded by a flurry of tiny hearts,
on it. "It's from Christina," she said. Jason and I were standing at
my locker, looking over an interview with Van Homan in the April
issue of *Transworld BMX*. It was spring of our sophomore year, and
I'd come close to asking a few girls out, but I couldn't get up the
nerve to do it. Jason snatched the note from my hand before I could
open it.

"Dear Ryan," he read in a mock Valley girl voice. "You're hot.
Do you want to be my boyfriend? Circle one: yes or no."

I grabbed it back from him, feeling a rush of heat in my cheeks.
His high-pitched laugh bounced off the lockers. "Don't you think
Christina's hot?" I asked. With her curly blonde hair, shopping mall
tan, and conspicuous thongs, pretty much every guy in school
lusted after her.

"Fuck...I don't know," Jason said. "She's okay. Seems like an
idiot, though."

"She gets perfect grades."

"Who cares?"

Against Jason's counsel, I circled yes and gave the note back
to Alissa after the next period. Using a silver metallic marker, she

wrote Christina's number on the back of my hand and told me to call that night.

On the phone, Christina and I nervously chatted for a few minutes before she finally said, "So...do you want to go out with me?"

My voice went hoarse for a second before I was able to cough out, "Yeah, sounds good."

She and Alissa, who was listening in, giggled. "Wow, so romantic," Alissa joked.

Jason and I were pretty disconnected from our peers, so I was surprised when Christina told me that she and Alissa had heard where we rode and parked on the street where Jason's house used to be. Apparently, they watched us ride, even though you couldn't see much from that spot. The thought of a girl seeking me out like that set loose a swarm of hummingbirds inside my chest.

I told Jason about my new relationship status when he picked me up for school the next morning. "Oh God, seriously? What the fuck are you gonna do, go to the mall with her?" I couldn't tell if he was jealous or what, but there was a sharpness to his tone.

He pretended not to care when I grabbed my Trapper Keeper from his locker and walked down the hall to meet up with Christina. For new couples, the first thing to do was walk around school holding hands to let everyone know what was up. Jason and I used to talk shit about the ritual, but, as I glanced at the light coat of glitter decorating Christina's shoulders and her heavily lip-glossed lips, I felt like a badass. Every guy I saw wished he was in my place. That feeling quickly morphed into embarrassment as a prodigious bulge appeared in my jeans. I stuffed my left hand in my pocket in a futile attempt to make my situation look less ridiculous.

For the first two weeks, that's what going out consisted of: walking around school holding hands and talking on the phone at night. I tried to play it cool with my parents, but they knew right away. To their credit, both Mom and Dad did their best not to tease me too much. Then, hanging out in the hall on a Thursday after school, Christina kissed me. I thought I was going to burst. On the phone that night, she told me to come over to her house on Saturday. She laughed and said, "We'll have the basement to ourselves. Oh yeah—bring Jason. Alissa thinks he's hot." I heard Alissa laugh in the background.

"I'm not going over there," Jason said while we waited in the lunch line the following day. "What would we even do?"

"What do you think, numbnuts?"

I had to do more coaxing than I'd anticipated to get him to Christina's house, especially considering that Alissa, with her pixie cut and curvy body, was a knockout. Jason drove us over in the Cutlass, parking in the street next to the front yard. The grass was mushy from melted snow. As I rang the doorbell of the formidable brick house, I still thought Jason might bolt and leave me hanging. He looked at his car, very clearly wanting to leave.

To our absolute horror, Christina introduced us to her parents after we took off our shoes and walked into the living room. Her dad was built like a linebacker and could've crushed me like an empty can. His arms and shoulders bulged beneath his flannel shirt, and he had a razor-shaved head. He said, "You're Danny Boy's son, right?" He shook my hand just a bit harder than necessary. Alissa and Christina watched us squirm like it was the funniest thing before we finally went downstairs.

"You guys like *Happy Gilmore?*" Christina put on the video, sat next to me, and then cranked the volume on the big screen. She'd been wearing a baggy gray sweatshirt, but she took it off to reveal a pink camisole. Next thing I knew, we were making out with the aggressive sloppiness of teenagers. I looked over at Jason, who was awkwardly holding Alissa's hand on the loveseat next to the TV. And then, like a character in a comic strip, I remember thinking, *Red alert! Red alert!* Before I could regain control of myself, I nutted in my jeans and hoped to God Christina didn't notice.

All I could say for myself was, "I gotta pee," which Christina and Alissa both thought was hilarious. Alissa immediately said, "I really gotta pee," in an annoyingly spot-on impersonation of Forrest Gump.

I ran the faucet in the bathroom and cleaned myself with toilet paper. When I came back out, I expected to see Jason and Alissa going at it. But they were glued to the same place, still just holding hands. They stayed like that until we left a few hours later.

The next weekend, I asked Christina if I should bring Jason again when I came over.

"Oh, didn't you hear? Alissa's going out with Steve now."

I only knew Steve as one of the punk rock kids, a band dude, but he seemed cool. It didn't matter anyway because it's not like we went to Christina's to hang out with each other. Jason seemed both relieved and pissed when I told him. "Who gives a fuck?" he said. "I'd rather jack off alone."

We usually didn't have to make plans with each other to ride the ramps in his mom's garage. Jason would just show up at my house to pick me up, and we'd go ride. So I felt like a jerk when he came over on a Thursday night, and I had to tell him I was about to leave. "Jesus Christ, dude," he said. "Do you even ride anymore?" Backing out of the driveway, he flipped me off and yelled, "Make sure you wear a rubber ya goddamn scallywag!" I flipped him off, too, which was both how we greeted each other and waved goodbye.

"Is Jason gay?" Alissa asked the next time she, Christina, and I were talking on the phone.

"What, if someone doesn't want to make out with you, they're automatically gay?" I shot back.

"Don't be a dick. It was just a feeling I got."

The thought had crossed my mind, but I knew better than to admit it to someone who'd spread it around a school that could be as backward as Suffield High. Another part of me didn't want it to be true for fear of how my dad would react.

The third time I went over to Christina's, she took me into her room. We did all the things teenagers are so eager to do, except, you know, THE BIG THING. I bragged to Jason about it the next time we rode in his garage. He flatly said, "Sounds intense," but didn't ask for any details.

Dudes at school hungrily asked me how far I'd gone with Christina. I initially tried to be guarded in what I told them—but then I was broadcasting all the details like an asshole. Christina found out immediately.

"You can trust me, I swear," I told her in a regret-filled fit of panic. "I'll never do anything like that again."

Alas, my pleas mattered naught: she was dating Kurt, the soccer player Jason and I mockingly called Captain Kurt, within a week. Ours was a spring relationship of only four weeks, but afterward, I dumbly felt like I understood the raw and relentless heartache bands like Glassjaw wrote entire records about.

Standing at his locker, I told Jason about Christina dumping me.

"You cried like a little bitch, didn't you?"

"Fuck off, no, I didn't."

"It's okay, darling. I'll never leave you." He faked like he was swooning into my arms. I dodged him and let him fall on his ass.

13

Our antics and pranks leveled up when we discovered Bam Margera's CKY (Camp Kill Yourself) videos, which were the blueprint for *Jackass*. We used to mess with each other like any close friends, but we became much more deliberate with our tomfoolery after watching those tapes. Between sporadic skating clips, Bam and his friends sat in shopping carts and pushed each other into curbs and bushes, laughing savagely and getting completely wrecked. Or they punched each other in the face from behind. Or they shocked each other with electric dog collars. Or they suggestively posed in tight underwear on the side of the road and filmed drivers' reactions.

You get the idea.

Riding big jumps is such an intense form of existence, it follows that our humor would become more intense along with our riding. Life at its normal pace was boring. I knew that was the case for Devin and his friends, too, as they were the ones to tell us about the CKY videos; but when I thought about hanging out with them in New York, that night still had a malicious tinge. I'd feel amped up as the memory played in my head, and I felt the most anxious when I thought of Trevor forcefully telling that girl to fuck Jason.

The snow had melted for the most part, but the dirt was still too wet to ride our jumps. We were hanging out at my house, watching the new FBM video for the umpteenth time, when I got an idea. "Let's film our own CKY video." For Christmas, Mom had bought Dad a new camcorder he never used. After a tense evening when he and Mom barely said a word to each other, I asked him if Jason and I could use it to film riding clips. "Yeah, whatever," he said, his mind clearly someplace else.

Without missing a beat, Jason said, "Go get the sour cream. I'll eat it in the shop, and you can film me puking."

I grabbed the camera from the computer room, then the sour cream and a wooden spoon from the kitchen. I couldn't stop giggling.

"What are you guys doing?" Mom was home early, grading papers at the dining room table. She looked at me over her glasses.

"Nothing, just messing around."

She shook her head but didn't stop me.

Jason and I went out back to my dad's shop. He wouldn't be home from work for a while yet. Even though he did his drinking in there, Dad kept the shop clean and in order. His white-and-blue Bronco was parked next to an old lathe he occasionally used. There was an enclosed tool room in the back corner. The walls were decorated with dated swimsuit posters and calendars. A spoof on a Budweiser ad, one poster read, "Buttweiser / King of Rears / Want's (sic) Your Bush" and featured three women's asses in thong bikinis with no other bodily context.

Jason sat on my dad's mini fridge and started shoveling sour cream into his mouth, gagging with each spoonful. I was laughing so hard, I could barely hold the camera. He began retching more violently. I grabbed an old bucket and set it at his feet. He waterfall-puked into it. He'd downed a Hawaiian Punch earlier, so his vomit was a horrible stream of white and pink. Strings of spittle dangled from his lips, and his eyes watered. He looked into the camera. We laughed our asses off.

Over the next few weeks, we kept one-upping each other's antics. My dad would blow a gasket if he caught us, so we filmed clandestinely. Part of me got a rush from doing things I knew would drive Dad up the wall, but I didn't want to tempt fate by doing pranks out in the open. I dove headfirst into a bush from the roof of the Cutlass while Jason was driving (slowly) and filming. He took his shirt off and let me whip his chest with a leather belt, leaving bright red welts. Slapping each other in the face from behind and filming the reaction became routine. In bed one night, I came up with an idea Jason wouldn't be able to top for a while.

The next afternoon, I pulled Mom's old mountain bike from the corner of the shop where it had been sitting for as long as I could remember, smirking when Jason asked what I was going to do.

"Just start filming," I said.

I wheeled the bike outside, its loose chain rattling. The driveway was still muddy in patches from the recently melted snow. I set the bike against the shop and went back in to grab a ladder.

Jason giggled and said, "Holy shit," when he realized what I was about to do.

I set up the ladder and climbed onto the roof. Jason lifted the mountain bike as high above his head as he could. My feet almost slipped off the edge as I crouched down, grabbed the front wheel, then swung the bike onto the roof. I got the mountain bike in position and put my left foot on the pedal, trying to psych myself up.

"You're not gonna do it," Jason said, pointing the camera at me.

"This is for Jesus Christ!" I yelled. "The one true patriot!"

Before I could stop myself, I pushed off, got in a half crank, and rolled off the roof. Knowing the mountain bike was front-end heavy, I pulled up as hard as I could. Just like when you hit a big double for the first time, there was a breathless, floating moment.

I landed back tire first and somehow rolled away, for a few feet at least. The rim folded in on itself upon impact, looking like a fucked-up taco shell made of cheap metal. Unable to go farther, I ghosted the bike into the basketball hoop. Between fits of laughter, Jason kept saying, "The one true patriot! The one true patriot!"

Once we got ahold of ourselves, I realized I needed to hide the bike before Mom or Dad came home because they'd both lose their shit if they saw it. I put the bike back in its place underneath the old PVC pipes and scrap wood in the shop, throwing a tarp over it for good measure. I was sure Dad would notice it that night, but he didn't.

I got another idea while playing Metal Gear Solid a few days after my mountain bike stunt. I told Jason I had to pee, and then I snuck into the kitchen instead and grabbed one of the glue mousetraps Dad kept under the sink. I got out the camera, turned it on, and snuck up behind Jason, who was concentrating on the game. Quick as a mongoose, I pressed the trap onto his cheek. I knew he thought mousetraps were nasty, but I didn't expect him to get as mad as he did. Looking at me like he wanted to murder me, his cheeks turned red, which only made it that much funnier. I ran to the other side of the living room. Pulling off the mousetrap, his cheek stretched out a few inches—then snapped back. I thought I might piss myself.

Jason chased me from one end of the house to the other, back and forth, glassware in the dining room cabinet shaking as we trampled through. We kept up the *Tom and Jerry* routine for a solid five minutes before he finally cornered me. I put my hands up to block him. Jason batted them away and slapped the trap onto my left cheek, pressing it on hard before I could get his arm away.

"You asshole, I didn't get you this bad." Jason just laughed and snatched the camera from me. I pulled on the trap, stretching my cheek until it hurt too badly. That thing was cemented onto my skin. It wouldn't budge. "It's stuck, you dipshit."

This, of course, only made it funnier to Jason.

I finally said fuck it and started pulling as hard as I could. My skin stretched like rubber—farther than you'd think possible. On video, it looked cartoonish, almost fake. When I finally yanked the trap off, my cheek felt slack, deflated. Jason laughed hysterically and kept filming. I balled up my right fist, on the verge of punching him. Instead, I started laughing, too, knowing the prank was going to make for choice footage.

By the time our jumps were rideable that year, we'd gotten bored with the *Jackass* video routine. I started feeling on edge all the time because I always had to look out for Jason to pull some shit on me. It was similar to the feeling I had around Devin and his friends.

14

During the summer I turned sixteen, we finished our third jump line: Orion. My parents bought me a gold S10 with only 30,000 miles and a camper shell, which meant I had to get my ass a job. I got hired at Suffield Hardware, where I sometimes stole spray paint so we could tag the ramps in Jason's garage.

With jobs and very little living expenses, we spent as much money on our bikes as we wanted. By then, I was riding a sky-blue S&M Stricker frame. Jason had a dark brown Terrible One, which, in all honesty, was always the best bike company. They simultaneously understood the art and absurdity of BMX, which was reflected in everything they did, from their pristine frames to the wacky little creatures on their shirts and stickers. When Jason built up his bike, I wished I'd followed my gut and gotten a T1, too. S&M was one of the most solid core companies—so the difference between our bikes was of coolness, not quality. We both bought sealed Profile cassette hubs and laced them onto double-walled Sun rims. We ran GT drop-nose seats (slammed, like Garrett Byrnes), Terrible One bars, and S&M Redneck stems. This stuff wasn't cheap. We'd spend hours in my dad's shop truing our wheels on the stand Jason made in his welding class—or meticulously examining our bikes to eke out any stray rattling or otherwise gross noise when we bounced our tires on the ground. Our bikes were finely tuned instruments, customized down to our semi-ironic skull-and-crossbones valve caps.

Jason's bike with me in the background

After riding one evening, I brought my bike into the shop, where I kept it, to find Dad hammered and listening to AC/DC. He used to shower and change clothes as soon as he got home from work, but lately, he didn't bother. He looked at me with bleary, unfocused eyes. "Let me see that thing," he said, grabbing my handlebars and yanking my bike from my hands. He rolled it back and forth, then scoffed. "It's a dead end, Ry. I know you expect Mommy and Daddy to pay for your college, but at least you could've helped if you'd stuck with basketball."

"You fucked it up for me. I used to like playing until you became a drill sergeant."

He took a step toward me but then wobbled on his feet, balancing himself on his mini fridge. Then, suddenly, he got choked up, turning his head away to hide it. "I love you, Ry; you know I do."

Truth is, I think my dad and I wanted the same thing: to be close to each other. We were both just so goddamn stubborn. Neither of us was willing to cede any ground to the other. That night in the shop could've been a meaningful moment for us, an opportunity to finally talk about how we really felt.

The next day, my dad acted like nothing happened. I don't know if he remembered it or not.

∿

Jason and I wanted Orion to be as impeccable as our bikes. It was our biggest line yet. When we were plotting the points where the lips and landings would go, and how it would tie into Battery and Harvester, I kept backing up with the wooden stakes. Jason motioned for me to go farther still.

"Dude, there's no way we'll be able to make this," I said. "Even if you can, by the end, you'll have so much speed you'll launch into the fucking tobacco."

"We just have to make the last jump bigger and steeper so you can air it higher."

I was typically the one who would be happier with building something more conservative, the Lars Ulrich of our duo. I pushed back against Jason's ideas even though he was usually right. I wouldn't have admitted it then, but he was the more ambitious rider.

Even as we put the finishing touches on the first and second jumps of Orion, I still wasn't convinced that we hadn't wasted two full weeks of digging. And then, with no warning, Jason came roaring down the path and glided off the first lip. His back end floated to the side as the leafy tendrils of a branch kissed his shoulder. No bullshit, he was at least twenty feet off the ground, if not more. It was higher than either of us had ever gone. Because he's Jason, he cranked a turndown over the second jump, which was about the most effective middle finger anyone had ever given me.

With an end in sight, we labored like coal miners. We dug with our shirts off, our lithe bodies slick with sweat. We came home with enough dirt in our hair, in our skin, and underneath our fingernails to stop up the drains. We'd rush home after work that summer and meet each other in the woods. Or, when one person had to work, the other would dig. I'd feel tired in my bones when I got home from the hardware store, but I'd wolf down dinner and force myself to go to the jumps, at which point the exhaustion seeped out in sweat that had actual purpose. Some people used Bobcats and similar machinery to build their trails. That would've felt wrong to us. All we needed were our shovels and wheelbarrow. We wanted to feel the weight of the dirt in our arms, watching how each individual shovelful contributed to the bigger picture.

One night, when Jason ate dinner with us, Dad said he couldn't understand why we'd do all that work by hand. I thought he was just being a jerk, but then he said, "I can't believe I'm offering, but if you boys want, I can rent a Bobcat and help you."

"We're good," I said quickly, slapping away the hand he'd offered. I didn't want my dad out there. It was a space that was supposed to be distant from him.

"Fine. It's your backs."

Digging the next morning, Jason said, "He just wants to connect with us, Ry. Let him help if he wants."

"He'll just get aggro and order us around. That's what he does." I stuck my shovel in the dirt. "Plus, you're the one who's always saying using tractors and shit like that is cheating."

Jason shook his head and said, "Whatever. Your call."

Within a week and a half, we finished the third jump in Orion and cleared, packed, and groomed the path to the last jump. Then we made the final jump taller, with a steeper lip and landing so it would function like a spine. You could go straight over if you weren't going fast enough, or you could air the fuck out of it, tracing a massive arc in the sky.

Jason ran the full line first (as always). At the bottom, he breathlessly told me to hit it, laughing from excitement. It was the first time I got scared shitless at our own trails. We're talking six-plus-foot jumps with twenty-plus-foot gaps by this point. Orion also contained the steepest downhill section in our woods. My guess would be that the line got you going around forty miles an hour, though we never clocked it. Forty miles an hour on a twenty-inch bike. I pedaled up to the first lip, acting like I hadn't gotten the feel by riding up it hundreds of times to pack it.

"It's not rocket science, Ry," Jason said. "Just pump and nosedive." He'd already walked his bike back to the top, ready for another run.

All of our jumps created that suspended-in-time, floating feeling you want. But goddamn, the first double in Orion made me feel like I was getting astral projected and then sling-shotted back to Earth. The lip shot me higher than my body anticipated, so I got butterflies as I ascended and swooped back down into the landing.

Ecstatic, we jumped the line again. And again. And again.

We felt as triumphant as a band who'd just tracked an unimpeachable album or a painter who'd completed a magnum opus. But if you would've described our feelings in those terms back then, we would've told you to eat a bag of shit.

Jason roasting Orion

15

A couple weeks after we finished Orion, I got it in my head that I'd try a three-sixty over the last set, even though I'd only done two-seventies over hips at Incline. Jason had been floating threes over it, spinning with an elegant, almost lazy rotation. I was still operating under the delusion that I could catch up to him if I pushed hard enough.

Knowing that most people loop out when they try threes for the first time, I nosedived too hard and cased the back of the landing with my front wheel. My bike clamored to the ground, the shrill *pings* upsetting the quiet of our woods. I got ejected, landing on my chest and sliding, baseball style, for a comical amount of time.

My right arm had gotten tucked under me at a weird angle—so yeah, my collarbone was nicely broken by the time Jason helped me up and brushed the dirt off my pants and shirt. Pain reverberated through my upper body. My arm dangled, hanging at a horribly low angle off my shoulder. Just the thought of moving my arm or shoulder hurt like a motherfucker. Not sure why, but every time I broke a bone riding, I yakked up everything in my stomach. My collarbone was no exception. I got up, walked a few steps, and then waterfall puked.

"You look like a ghost," Jason said. He couldn't help himself from laughing a bit. I would've done the same thing.

ᔕᕗ

I'm sure this will sound melodramatic, but having an injury when your entire identity is based on riding fucking sucks. It was a lot of that buzzing restlessness you feel when you have to work or study, but there's this other, *way better* thing you'd rather be doing, whether it's going to a concert, or on a trip, or getting fucked by someone who likes you back.

When the doctor set my bone, I thought I might throw up again. I must've looked like I was going to because he said, "I can get you a vomit tray if you need."

I was about to tell him I was good when my mom said, "That would be great, thank you."

In the days after, my collarbone didn't hurt all that much unless I tried to move my right shoulder, at which point it hurt more than any injury I'd endured, a deep ache that echoed like a scream in a cavern. The bone wasn't broken badly enough to need surgery, though. I just had to keep my arm in a sling. I wore T-shirts without putting my right arm through the sleeve, leaving my appendage to dangle under a blob of fabric. I had to basically shuffle into a shirt every morning and then shuffle back out the next day when I took a shower, all the while hoping I didn't move my arm in a painful way.

My boss at the hardware store invented nonsense things for me to do while I was hurt, like double-checking the hammer inventory he'd already memorized, which was honestly better than hanging out at home and playing *Tony Hawk's Pro Skater* or watching *Dogtown and Z-Boys* or my six BMX videos for the thousandth time.

After about two weeks of me moping around the house, Mom bought me a copy of Kem Nunn's *Tapping the Source*, the surf-noir masterpiece that inspired *Point Break*. That was part of her brilliance as a teacher: She could find exactly the right book to capture your interest, which was no easy feat when it came to moody teenagers.

"You'll like this one" was all she said when she set the book next to me on the sofa.

Even though Nunn's subject was surfing, there were these great sections in *Tapping the Source* that gave shape and language to so many thoughts I had about riding trails. He talked about surfing as this elemental activity, a communion with nature. The better you got, the deeper the connection. When you weren't surfing, he wrote, you were reading the waves and weather. Jason and I had gotten to the point where we could read how much moisture was in the dirt with only a passing glance. Trails involved a different level of the mechanical compared to surfing, as the obstacles didn't simply exist in nature, not without humans and tools. Even so, it felt like a deeply truthful way of connecting with the woods and soil. There were those New Age people who talked a lot about nature's calm, but nature always seemed fucking gnarly to me. A human life could get snuffed out so easily by endless things in the mountains, ocean, forest, or desert. Brushing up against the fear of death and pushing past it was a way of honoring that gnarliness. It's true: this is the language of reflection, but these ideas were there, spinning around in my brain. When I tried to talk to Jason about this stuff, he'd say, "I don't know, dude, I just like to ride my bike."

He stopped by my house every time he went to the trails, although neither of us rode as much if the other was injured, at least back then. That restless feeling was way worse in our woods. I'd take photos and film, but the best I could hope for was a few seconds of dissociation—so I could pretend it was me doing picture-perfect three-sixty tables over the last jump. As Jason laid his bike down flat, mid-spin, the world seemed to pause.

We also spent a lot of time at Jason's, playing *Pro Skater* and watching videos. Laurie babied us more than my mom when we were injured. It's not like Mom was mean about it. She just didn't pity us as much for getting hurt doing this incredibly dangerous thing we knew was incredibly dangerous. My dad had no sympathy whatsoever for BMX injuries, just irritation for having to pay the medical bills.

"There's my boys," Laurie would say when we walked into their small yellow house.

They had a very fat orange cat named Jeeves. No one except for Jason or Laurie could pet that little bastard. Laurie liked to burn incense. The smell of their house reminded me of a Hot Topic store. Their maroon shag carpet collected smoke, so the waxy incense odor was always strong. There were pictures of Scott everywhere—of his and Laurie's wedding (they both looked great with feathered hair); of the family at the races with Jason standing next to a trophy taller than him; of Scott's life before Laurie and Jason came along, when he raced motocross. In one, he held up a second-place trophy and smiled triumphantly from behind the same exact handlebar mustache he had when I knew him. His shaggy black hair was matted down from sweat, and his helmet hung on the grip of his mud-spattered motorcycle. The resemblance between him and Jason was striking.

Scott had an autographed photo of Hank Williams (Sr.) that his dad had given him. It sat in the middle of the shelf that lined the wall behind the TV. His name scrawled in the upper left corner, Hank looked at you with a bright exuberance that contrasted with his depressive songs. Scott was just such a rad guy. I still found myself crying for him from time to time, like when I'd hear a Sabbath or AC/DC song on the radio. Along with a bunch of Jason's trophies, Laurie's AA tokens lined the shelf where they kept Scott's ashes and his photo of Hank Williams.

When we watched videos, Laurie would watch, too, cringing during the crashes, saying the riders were dumbasses for not wearing helmets, calling them assholes during the party scenes, and practicing her BMX vernacular. "Clickback!" she said, excitedly. "Right, J?" Sitting next to us on their fur-covered couch, she gave Jeeves, that villain, a scratch under his jaw.

"Lookback."

"Oh, same goddamn thing. But when someone does that one right, they click it." She sat in the groove Scott had worn into the couch so long ago. It was only recently that Laurie or Jason would sit there.

"Nice, Mom."

In addition to multiple tricks, Laurie recognized Posh when people rode it. Every time we saw footage of it, Jason and I talked about it like it was our holy land.

16

It felt like years at the time, but I was mostly healed up within a month and a half. My collarbone hurt when I rode, but I forced myself to push past the pain. Devin had been telling us to come ride Posh since the snow melted. When I broke my collarbone, I had this huge fear that it would take me out of commission for the entire summer. Jason wouldn't have gone alone, but he might've dragged my ass down there if I was still unable to ride. We made it by the end of August, when it was as hot and humid as Satan's asshole.

Jason and I hadn't talked much about our New York trip aside from how sick it was to watch Edwin and those guys ride street. We tried to laugh the rest of it off. It was just the type of humor we had to get used to if we were going to become elite riders.

We were giddy because we were going to Posh, but there was also some negative energy with us as we drove to Bethlehem. We were going to hang out with Devin and his friends again, and this time around, we had more of a sense of who they really were. My anxiety was not alleviated by Jason playing Eyehategod's *Take as Needed for Pain* at full volume. There was definitely something about those huge, crushing riffs and knuckle-dragging drums that connected to the death-drive effortlessness of riding big trails. There was also this wretched misanthropy that, if we weren't listening to it while riding, made my stomach tight. Jason listened to Eyehategod all the time, though. When something scared him, he wanted to confront it. My instinct was often to slink away. I needed other riders to push me. Whether he was alone or with other people, Jason rode with the same abandon.

Devin had given us the address of a church near Posh where we could park my truck, so we met him there and then pedaled a few blocks to the trails. We cut across a narrow path through dense woods—then there it was. You know the feeling of standing at the foot of a mountain or the precipice of a canyon and realizing how tiny and insignificant you are? That's how it felt seeing Posh for the first time.

We knew the jumps would be bigger than they looked on video, but Christ, these looked like motorcycle doubles. Snaking berms led into rollers that led into hips that led into straight hits from which you could transfer to three different lines, each with its own unique outcome. And this shit was faultless, looking like some marble/dirt hybrid that had been sculpted by renegade artisans. Vines and grass reached up the sides of jumps. An army of trees guarded it from the outside world.

Posh, 2000

There were more people than I'd expected, both riding and just hanging out, drinking beer and smoking weed off to the side. It was not what you would call a welcoming vibe. The first time I watched *Deliverance* a few years later and the scene came on where the cocky outsiders got stared down by surly hill folk, I remember saying to my girlfriend, *"That's* how it felt to show up at Posh for the first time."

Guys who weren't zipping through the lines stared at us like, *Who the fuck are you?* There's no question in my mind that we would've gotten our asses kicked if Devin hadn't brought us. The energy became a lot different when Posh went public. At the time, though, that clip in *Seek & Destroy* of the mountain bike kid getting punched in his dome played on repeat in my brain.

"Speedball is a good line to get warmed up on. Just don't fuck up the landings," Devin said with a smirk.

"Neb will fuck your mouth if you mess anything up," Trevor added.

Jason and I awkwardly tried to laugh with them.

Devin ran Speedball to show us, gliding through like it was second nature. It was obvious by the way he pumped that he knew those trails intimately.

Thank fuck Jason went before me, and not only that—he made it most of the way through Speedball first try, veering off at the last jump. My hands shook before I pushed off, but I managed not to tense up in the air. I made it the same distance as Jason and immediately realized why he didn't get all the way through. There was this little troll roller you had to know about and pump right before the last double, or else it would eat all your speed. It was yet another way of telling people who didn't know how to ride to get the fuck out. We both made it through the next try. The lips, landings, and angles were absolutely perfect. If you trusted yourself enough to surrender to the flow and momentum of the trails, they essentially jumped themselves. The tension in the air drained out when everyone saw how we rode—when they knew we weren't going to denigrate their hard work.

My initial unease at seeing Neb and Trevor morphed into awe as I watched them flow through each line, alone and in trains with each other. The zip of their tires as they launched off each lip was as piercing as an eagle's peal. A lot of the guys were shirtless, which seemed like a bold move given how fast they were going and how hard-packed the jumps were. Their bodies glistened with sweat.

Neb blasting Speedball

"Get in this one with us," Trevor said as several guys chased after each other, nearly touching tires. I followed Jason, who slipped in at the last quarter of the train. Neb came in behind me, this momentous mass making me nervous about being the one to crash and derail it all. But then I let go and lost myself in the train's rhythm, becoming part of this singular worm making its triumphant crawl across the earth.

Last part of a Posh train—Jason in front, Trevor in back

It all felt so pure, but anxiety gripped my lungs later that evening when Devin asked if we wanted to party at Chunk House, where a bunch of riders, including himself, lived. We obviously weren't going to say no.

Located in a fairly quiet neighborhood about ten minutes from Posh, Chunk House was somewhat dilapidated on the outside, but not as bad as you'd expect. Inside, it was basically a punk house but BMX style. The walls were painted dark green and gray, alternating at random. Posters for underground punk and metal bands like

Combatwoundedveteran and Floor were plastered up. There was an old TV and VCR in the front room. A GG Allin video played, and there he was with his little cocktail wiener dick, yelling into a microphone and making angry gestures. I didn't know much about him, other than he used to take shits on stage and throw it at people. Some years later, I saw the footage of him on *Jerry Springer*, the footage where Allin said that if a rape happened at one of his shows, it was simply part of the show.

A bunch of guys were hanging out on the back porch, drinking High Life and smoking cigarettes and weed. Most of them had shaggy hair and tight pants. Devin asked if we wanted a beer. Everyone was eyeing us, but there were a few other kids our age, so we didn't feel completely out of place. Two or three scene girls were hanging out, and it was the same story as almost every BMX party I've been to: several guys lurking around them, trying to get laid.

The guys at Chunk House all rode beautifully, by the way. So when multiple of them complimented Jason on his turndowns and threes, and me on my tables and X-ups, it meant something. These weren't people who gave compliments to other riders unless it was deserved. They were impressed with me, but they were smitten with Jason's riding. Him outshining me was old hat by then. I was still jealous.

When I think of these parties, there was this mellow before period where everyone was hanging out and chatting, usually pretty tired from riding. And then, in the blink of an eye, shit would get wild. The music would get louder, and you'd see guys putting each other in headlocks, shotgunning beers, and, if there were any around, shooting bottle rockets and Roman candles at each other. It always turned into a version of *Jackass*—but you were there, so you couldn't change the channel. It was more menacing than when

Jason and I would pull pranks on each other. For these guys, there was a desire to cause real pain.

I felt a warmth on the back of my neck before I finished one beer. Looking at Jason laughing and playing air guitar to Sabbath, I knew he did, too. I think we both had two more, but it's hard to remember. What I do remember is Devin and Neb taking turns punching each other in the chest to see who could knock the other one down. They reared back and did exaggerated windups, their fists landing with meaty thuds and unhinged laughter. They had their shirts off, so their chests were decorated with red splotches. The women at the party left soon after.

At one point, Devin poured nail polish remover on his flaccid dick and, while someone filmed, lit it on fire for a few seconds. He looked into the camera right before touching the match to his skin. That clip ended up in the credits of *Criminal Mischief*. We all laughed hysterically.

Another thing I remember is when Devin asked Jason and me if we were virgins, if we'd ever fucked a girl. I told him about my exploits with Christina. Jason still hadn't kissed anyone, so he stayed quiet.

"You guys want to jack off with us?" Devin asked as he, Trevor, Neb, and some other guys giggled. He said it so offhandedly, I was sure he was fucking with us. Jason and I looked at each other and then back at him, unsure what to say. "If it's just with your friends," Devin said, "it's not gay." They all thought this was the funniest thing. "Well, maybe it is, but who gives a fuck."

At the time, it made perfect sense: we were a bunch of young guys who were masturbating all the time anyway, so why not lend each other a hand? Looking back, it's so clear that the BMX world throbbed with homoeroticism, from the way we acted and looked at each other to the way we talked. Fooling around was an extension of that.

I got hard instantly; but I still hesitated, not knowing if we should.

"I'm down," Jason said, getting up from the couch. He reached out to me. I grabbed his hand, and he pulled me up.

We went into a messy bedroom where Devin set a dirt-encrusted towel on the ground. "First one to shoot gets a punch in the dick," he said, a jokester to the end. Guys surrounded the towel and unzipped their pants, pulling down their boxers to reveal already-hard cocks of varying sizes and shapes. Most of them had hair on their stomach and thighs, much more than me or Jason. A few of them spit on their hand before they started. A few of them helped each other. I unbuckled my belt but hesitated again—until I saw Jason's Dickies and underwear around his ankles.

Whenever I heard Dad or one of the football coaches at school say, "What is this, a circle jerk?" I never thought of it as a literal thing. But there we were, standing in a circle and, after what seemed like seconds, relieving ourselves onto a dirty white towel alongside our heroes.

∿

Driving home the next day, I don't think Jason or I knew whether we should be proud or ashamed. We didn't know how to talk about what happened. So we didn't. In the weeks to come, I couldn't stop thinking about it, replaying every detail on a loop. I'd zone out at work and come to with my boss snapping his fingers and saying, "Earth to Ryan." I also started having dreams where I'd see Devin, Trevor, and Neb's laughing faces. I'd jolt up in bed, covered in sweat.

Part of my anxiety stemmed from the fact that I had no template for bisexuality, a way to make sense of the fact that, yes, I genuinely did think lots of girls at school were extremely hot, and there was no ambiguity to that side of my lust. But now, here was this other side that felt really good, even though I hadn't thought consciously of another guy in that way before. In my head, the question that kept coming up over and over was, "Does this mean you're gay?" And then I'd say to myself, "But you do like girls, too, right? Or is that just you hiding?" Somewhere in me, I knew the last part was paranoia and shame. It was all so fucking confusing. Of course I'd heard of bisexuality, but the only versions I'd seen were when women would drunkenly make out on reality TV or in porno mags where the threesome scenarios always revolved around straight male fantasy.

It's so obvious that I needed guidance, someone to say, "Yes, it's entirely possible to be attracted to both women and men. It's also possible to favor one over the other while still wanting to enjoy both. There's nothing wrong with those feelings." Instead, we had a bunch of grown men, many of whom had been alive for at least a decade longer than us, chortling and asking if we wanted to jack off onto a towel.

We came back to Posh twice more that year, and it was a variation of the same thing. We also rode Catty Woods, another set of legendary trails only twenty minutes away. Not only were we accepted as legit riders by guys who built some of the best jumps on Earth (we were especially badass because we were young shredders), but now we'd been invited into their secret world.

The morning after our second group experience, Jason said, "I know people at school would think we're gay, but it's honestly not a big deal." We were driving home and had stopped at a gas station. He popped a handful of M&Ms in his mouth.

I drove back onto the highway. My heart started beating faster, but I just said, "Yeah, seriously. They'd blow it way out of proportion. It's no different than jacking off alone."

"I mean, maybe it would be gay if it was with some random dudes," Jason said. "But it's just part of the trail scene. Guys in the Navy do the same thing when they're out at sea."

I've heard a few riders look back and say, by way of explanation, that bisexuality was just trendy at the time. But telling me that would've done nothing to untangle the twine ball of anxiety that relentlessly pinged the bones inside my chest.

17

Back home, I collapsed on the sofa, feeling like every ounce of energy had been extracted from my body. I woke up to my dad's irate face hovering above me. His Brut aftershave startled my nostrils. The edges of his goatee were perfectly straight, as if he'd used a ruler when he trimmed it. "You reek of booze," he said.

"I don't drink. I thought you knew that."

"Oh, right. Then you won't mind coming out to the yard and doing some sprints with me."

"Go for it," I said, lying back on the sofa and turning away from him.

"I wasn't asking," he said, grabbing me by the shoulder and pulling me up to a sitting position. "Let's go. You're going to sweat that shit out."

I very nearly told him to fuck off. Instead, I said, "You get tanked every night. You can't get mad at me for doing the same thing."

"Let's go," he said, yanking my arm.

"Jesus, fuck. Fine."

All I could see in that moment was my dad's absurd hypocrisy. If I'd looked a bit closer, I would've seen that he didn't want me to drink because, even though he wouldn't have admitted it, he knew he had a problem with alcohol—because both his dad and grandpa had the same problem—and, despite his tendency to drown his brain in beer, he wanted that cycle to stop with me. I just thought he was trying to punish me for being different than him. I also wondered if he somehow knew what Jason and I did the previous night at Chunk House, as if he could peer inside my mind and excavate secrets.

My legs felt like they were filled with gravy as I followed him out the door to the front yard. "To the driveway and back," he said, nodding in that direction.

All of a sudden, I was ten years old again and mindlessly obeying him when he'd make me run drills. I jogged to my truck and back, feeling an acidic burn crawl up my throat.

"Bullshit," Dad said. "You look like you're late for the short bus. Let's go again."

His words broke my trance. "I can still beat your fat ass, even hungover."

"Let's see it then," he said. He told me where to line up. "To your truck and back. On the count of three."

On three, I lunged past him and ran a few yards but then stopped dead in my tracks as vomit gushed from my mouth and nose. My dad ran by me like nothing happened, stopping past the walkway to the front door, where we'd started. "Atta girl," he said. "I knew running would get it out."

I wiped brownish-orange spittle from my nose and chin. "Let's go again," I said, suddenly feeling like it was VERY IMPORTANT to show my dad that I could run faster than him. Dad counted off again. My throat and lungs still burning, I ran harder than I had since I was a kid, blasting past him and then, after touching my truck, looking him in the eye on my way back.

"Best two out of three," he said, breathing hard but trying not to show it.

I beat him again, feeling the same stupid rush of pride. Somewhere in each of us was a real desire to mend our frayed bond, but it mutated into something ugly and useless on its way to the surface, leaving us to charge at each other like apes.

After winning the last race, I threw up again, this time into the bush next to the doorstep.

18

"Let's just try it, dude. It will be fun," Jason said. He'd picked me up in the Cutlass, and we were waiting in the drive-thru line at Wendy's. We always said we knew our jumps well enough to ride them in the dark, but we were only boasting. Jason actually wanted to ride them at night with little runner's lights attached to our handlebars. It was the fall of our junior year. We spent every free moment at our trails, riding them as much as possible before winter.

"I don't know, J…It seems too gnarly."

"Devin and Trevor told me they do it all the time."

"Aren't you scared to eat shit?" I asked.

"It's all muscle memory at this point. Your body will know what to do." I handed him five bucks for my food. He parked in the oil-stained lot, and we ate in his car. We didn't like to eat inside because we always saw someone from school in there.

"Fuck…it does sound fun," I said, dipping a fry in my Frosty.

He brought it up a few more times over the next week, eventually talking me into it. We bought some running lights at the sporting goods store and tied the elastic bands to our crossbars. We each took a few laps through Battery during the day to make sure the lights wouldn't fall off. The trees were speckled with yellow, orange, and red.

Jason stayed at my house that night. Waiting for my parents to turn out the lights and go to bed, I felt giddy, like we were twelve all over again and waiting to sneak out to play ding dong ditch. We hung out in my dad's shop to pass the time, acting like we were working on our bikes.

We waited for a half hour after the lights in the house went out to make sure my parents were asleep. Then we donned our hoodies and headed out. Gravel crunched beneath our tires as we rode across the driveway to the skinny path that led to our woods. We kept pedaling so our ticking freewheels wouldn't wake up my parents. Once we were far enough away, we let our bikes' buzz fill the quiet Connecticut night. An owl hooted somewhere nearby, its voice carrying over the din of crickets. A slight but portentous chill laced the air.

We got to the tree line and turned on our lights. Our jumps were newly intimidating at night—dark, featureless monoliths that suddenly seemed strange and unfamiliar. Fireflies flitted about, little globules of light mapping out the ether. I pictured myself running off-course and slamming into a tree. It's never good when you clearly visualize a wreck. The fear in your body becomes rigid.

"Shit. I don't know about this, J."

Jason went to the top and, after hesitating only a second, started gliding through Battery. All you could see was the light on his handlebars—rising, falling, turning, moving forward. His tires hummed in the branches. Over the last jump, his light turned toward me and then snapped back as he did an X-up.

Jason laughed at the bottom. "Do it, Ry," he said, breathing heavily. "Just don't think about it."

Goddamnit. I walked my bike to the top of the path and found our starting point. I put my foot on my pedal but then paused.

"For real. Don't think about it," Jason said.

"I can barely see the lip."

"Your body knows the jumps. Trust me."

I pushed off without giving myself another chance to hesitate. As I glided off the first lip and pushed my front wheel into the landing, fear left my body. The light gave you just enough of a sense of where you were to allow muscle memory to take over. I pumped straight through the line, adding none of Jason's flourishes. Next thing I knew, my light was shining on leafy tobacco plants. Riding trails, you had to turn off your conscious mind to a certain extent. This was ripping the chord from the wall.

We each ran it one more time. After the second time through, even Jason didn't want to press our luck. It was the type of thing other riders would've bragged about, but neither of us felt the need. We kept it to ourselves. It was simply this beautiful thing that happened—and it was ours, no one else's.

Back in my room, our hearts pounding too hard to fall asleep, Jason put his hands on my body, and I put mine on his.

19

When someone told me there was a new kid at school named Tanner, I didn't think much of it—not until I saw him walking down the hall next to the gym. He was tall and muscular with shaggy blond hair, and he was wearing a green S&M shirt and Little Devil cargo pants.

"You ride?" I asked him.

"Yeah, dude," Tanner said. "I just moved up from the city with my parents. I used to ride with Ralph Sinisi and the Animal guys all the time."

"That's rad! We met Edwin and Vic not too long ago."

Meeting a like-minded soul in a place like Suffield was the equivalent of finding an envelope of $100 bills on the ground. I excitedly told Jason about Tanner at lunch.

"Let's get him to the jumps," he said.

I saw Tanner at his locker and asked if he wanted to ride our trails after school. He seemed nervous all of a sudden. "I used to ride dirt all the time, but I like street a lot more now." He shook his hair out to make it look shaggier.

"Yeah...there's not much street around here," I said.

He paused for a second, then said, "Fuck it. I'll come check out your jumps."

"It'll be easier to show you where they are if I pick you up. Where's your house?"

I drove over with Jason that afternoon. Tanner's house was essentially a mansion: a massive white three-story with bay windows that looked out onto a spacious back porch and ornate garden. Jason said, "Fuck, he's even richer than you, Ry."

Tanner opened the garage door and wheeled out his bike. He had a brown Garrett Byrnes T1 frame decked out with every part Profile made. It was a $2,000 bike, at least. I got out and helped him put it in the flatbed of my truck. The bike looked brand-new, with no wear and tear on any of the parts.

Tanner squeezed in next to Jason. "Thanks for asking me to ride, you guys."

"Fuck yeah," Jason said. "That's a badass bike. Ry mentioned that you know the Animal guys?"

"Yeah, I used to ride with Ralph."

"You ever ride the Brooklyn Banks?" I asked, backing out of the driveway. "That shit's nuts."

"That's one of my favorite spots," Tanner said.

His stomach dropped when he saw our jumps—you could see it on his face. "Oh damn, these are, like, legit trails," he said. "I might just watch you guys."

"Fuck that, they look way worse than they are," Jason said. He looked at me, then back to Tanner, making no effort to hide his sneer. "You got it."

Jason and I ran Battery and Harvester a few times. Just to be a dick, Jason three'd every jump in Harvester. "Let's see it, beefcake," he said, looking at Tanner like he was a wind-up toy. "You can at least hit one jump."

"I don't know, man. These are the biggest trails I've ever seen."

"Just the first jump in Battery. Don't be a bitch," Jason said.

"You got that first one," I said. "It's easy."

It's true: we were assholes. Tanner was obviously terrified, but we wouldn't leave him alone. He finally walked his bike to the top of the path. His bike was professional-grade, but he didn't know how to take care of it. His chain bounced on his frame, and something in his headset jingled. I let out a dickhead guffaw as he shakily put his right foot on the pedal, trying to pump himself up.

"Let's do it to it, brother!" Jason yelled, hamming up his Arkansas accent, which was normally faint, and pumping his fist in the air.

Tanner kicked off and got in an awkward pedal. He launched, cockeyed, off the lip—and sank like a baby bird kicked out of its nest. His front wheel made it to the landing, but his rear wheel hung off the back. His sprocket cut into the dirt, taking a huge gash out of our groomed landing. Under normal circumstances, Jason and I would've been pissed. But this was too funny. Somehow, Tanner didn't get wrecked.

"Oh wow, brother, just wow," Jason said. "You really caught some air there." I couldn't help myself from giggling.

Tanner walked his bike down to where we were standing. Chunks of dirt were caked in the spaces of his chain.

"Yeah, brother," I said, "I almost came in my jeans."

Tanner tried to laugh along with us, but he'd become our unwitting clown, and he knew it. He tried to hit the jump one more time, much to the same result. When we dropped him off at his house later, Tanner had a tight expression on his face, like he'd gotten caught whacking it in the school bathroom.

A couple days later, I invited him to ride our jumps again. Tanner drove over in his dad's forest-green Land Rover. He was feeling braver this time around. He decided he was going to hit the first jump of Harvester, despite it being bigger than the first jump of Battery. He watched Jason and I run the line a few times, then he walked his bike to the top, paused for a second, and pedaled toward the jump. Instead of pumping, he kept pedaling through the rollers, which threw off his balance before he even reached the jump. Jason and I laughed hysterically.

Tanner at least had sense enough to bail. He went off the lip at a grotesque angle, hopping off his bike and landing on his feet. Meanwhile, his bike slammed into a tree, clanking pitifully to the ground.

Jason and I were practically pissing ourselves.

We rode for another twenty minutes or so while Tanner sat at the bottom and watched, cheering us on, which cut through my ironic detachment and actually made me feel bad. I'd brought a little boombox out to the jumps in my backpack. Jason put in an Eyehategod CD.

"Whoa, this sounds crazy," Tanner said. "Who is this?"

"It's Captain Hand Job and the Twinks," Jason said, chortling.

"For real, who is it?" Tanner flipped his hair out of his eyes and looked at Jason.

"For real," Jason said. "The band is called Captain Hand Job and the Twinks."

"Whatever." Tanner went over to the boombox to see for himself. I thought it was funny, but I also wondered why Jason couldn't just tell him it was Eyehategod. I thought we should ease up on the kid, at least a bit.

After we took a few more runs, Jason said, "Hey, Tan the Man, you ever jack off one of your friends?"

Since that night in my room, Jason and I had been giving each other hand jobs in the woods. We'd stand next to each other and compare, and, when we argued about whose was bigger, we measured. When we were alone, it felt different than with the Posh guys, like it was less of a joke. There was an added gravity neither of us knew how to deal with. It went without saying that we didn't talk about this with anyone else.

I glared at Jason. It didn't seem worth it to reveal this side of our lives just to fuck with someone. "Don't listen to him," I said to Tanner. "He's kidding."

"Ry's just being shy." Jason looked right at me. "We do it with the Posh guys, too."

"Bullshit, no you don't. You're fucking with me again."

"No, man, for real. We like to jack each other off," Jason said.

"Let's just ride, J," I said. "It's a stupid joke." My cheeks felt hot.

Tanner eyed Jason, still trying to gauge if he was joking. Somewhere between Jason's prodding and me trying to get him to shut the fuck up, Tanner realized Jason was serious about our sexual escapades. He said he had to get home for dinner. He rode to my parents' driveway and drove off in his dad's SUV. We knew he'd never come back.

∿

It didn't take long for the story to get around school. I knew Jason hadn't considered this consequence when he was screwing with Tanner, but I was still pissed at him. As it turns out, Tanner was a talented soccer player, so he fell in with Captain Kurt and the bro crowd. He stopped wearing BMX shirts, instead coming to school decked out like an Abercrombie & Fitch model.

All our classmates soon knew what Jason and I did. You could tell by the way they looked at us or how they would stop talking when either of us walked into a room. We denied Tanner's story when anyone asked, but it didn't matter. At Suffield High, two guys fooling around with each other was Grade-A gossip.

Surrounded by his new crew, Tanner walked by us in the hall about a month after he came to our jumps and said, "Why don't you hold hands, you little fags?" Captain Kurt and his cronies laughed.

After they walked away, I told Jason, for what felt like the hundredth time, that he shouldn't have said anything to Tanner.

"I was just trying to fuck with him." He kept his eyes on the ground.

"Whatever," I said, grabbing my books from my locker. "Nothing we can do about it now."

I had English class with Christina and a few of her friends later in the day. When we were supposed to be quietly reading a chapter from *Dracula*, Christina whispered, loud enough for me to hear, "I can't believe I was ever with him. It's disgusting. Alissa knew right away they do gay stuff together."

I could feel my face redden, but I acted like I didn't hear her, like I didn't know she wanted me to hear her. I told Jason about it at our trails that evening.

"Fuck all those people," he said, gripping his handlebars tightly. "They're just a bunch of yokel morons. They'll never leave Suffield. They're going nowhere."

We took a brief hiatus from fooling around with each other, but within a matter of weeks, we were back at it, forgetting, if only for a few minutes, that according to everyone at school, we should be ashamed of making each other feel this way.

20

As soon as the snow stuck, Jason and I started riding the ramps in his mom's garage again. My dad knew about them, but he didn't see our cut-rate quarter pipes until he came over to give Laurie some venison from a deer he had recently killed.

Looking at the plywood-grafted transitions, he said, "These look like trash. I could've done better when I was in grade school."

Of course he had to make some cutting remark. Over dinner that night, he said, "I don't see how those piece-of-shit ramps are even standing." He chuckled as if he'd said something clever.

"Let us build a ramp in your shop, then."

"No fucking way. I need the space."

"For what, all the beer cans?"

He gripped his fork like he wanted to stab me with it. Before he responded, my mom cut in. "Why don't you let them? What would it hurt?"

"We'll keep it in the back, next to the old pipes and scrap wood," I said. "It won't take up hardly any space."

My dad stared through me, knowing full well I'd taken advantage of the situation. Then he looked at Mom with softened eyes, almost audibly hoping this could heal something between them. He sighed, looked back at me, and said, "If you screw anything up, I'm using your ramp for firewood."

"We'll be careful."

"I'm serious. I want that shop to be pristine."

My mom smiled to herself, spinning her fork on her plate to pick up an extra bite of spaghetti. I'm sure, like Dad, she noticed that I'd been hungover when I got back from my trips to Bethlehem. I thought I was being sneaky, but I probably smelled like a tavern ashtray. Prescription opiates were beginning to ravage communities on the East Coast, and Mom had watched several of her students at the middle school fall into that pit. If Jason and I were busy building and riding ramps in Dad's shop, she wouldn't have to worry about us drinking and popping Oxys to escape the boredom of winter.

I called Jason after dinner to tell him my dad was going to let us build a quarter pipe in the shop. He said, "Your mom made him do it, didn't she?"

The next day, I picked Jason up and drove over to Suffield Lumber. Snow creaked beneath the tires of my truck when I slowed at the intersections. Jason and I both had money saved from our jobs. We were more than happy to blow it on wood for a new ramp. We had these stupid grins on our faces as we bought hundreds of dollars' worth of two-by-fours, plywood, and eight-by-tens. We piled the lumber in the back of my truck, our breath becoming white wisps in the frigid air.

After unloading the wood into the shop, Jason and I got to work. Ramp building was much easier with my dad's high-end tools and the right materials. We spent all day and well into the evening making measurements, cutting wood with the table saw, and drilling everything together. The concrete floor was covered in a thick coat of sawdust.

During an afternoon break, Mom came in to check our progress. "Looks great, guys. Or wait, I'm supposed to say, 'Totally rad, dude.'" She talked in her best surfer voice and made the hang loose sign. It was a corny joke, even for Mom. "You two better be wearing helmets in here." As with every other time she told us to wear helmets, we said we would with no intention of doing so. We only wore them at indoor skateparks where it was required.

By that first night, we'd finished the full skeleton of our new quarter pipe. All we had to do the next day was drill a few layers of plywood down, which we did first thing in the morning. Compared to constructing ramps, there was something more intimate about building trails that had to do with the way the dirt got in our hands and hair, with how it stuck to our tires when we rolled up a lip dozens of times to pack it. But as Jason and I aired the quarter and messed around with coping tricks, I felt a giddiness similar to when we finished a new line in the woods. There was something else, too: we'd carved out a space for ourselves in my dad's shop, that fortress of manliness. It was exhilarating.

We spent all day riding the ramp. We lined up next to the door and sprinted past the lathe and Bronco, hit the quarter, and then rode back on the same narrow path of obstruction-free concrete. Jason put an Eyehategod CD in my dad's stereo and blasted it, the sludgy guitar notes clinging to the walls and oozing down. We started going higher, almost hitting our heads on the roof.

The session was heating up—but then my dad came in, robbing the air of energy. I could immediately tell by his heavy breathing that he was drunk. The day before, he and Mom had gotten in a screaming match about Jason and I building our quarter pipe, so I wasn't surprised to see him in this state.

Dad closed the door and stomped snow off his steel-toe boots. The acrid beer smell rushed in along with the cold. "What's this screaming crap?" he said about the music. "The riffs sound like Sabbath, but the singer sounds like he's got a ferret in his ass."

For as much of an asshole as my dad could be, I couldn't deny that he could also be pretty damn funny sometimes. Jason and I looked at each other and laughed.

"Let's see it, girls," Dad said, waving his hand at the ramp.

Jason pedaled hard at the quarter, like he was blasting out of the gate in a race, and aired a full six feet above the coping, locking his bike horizontally in a perfect tabletop. Freestyle was subjective, open to interpretation, and individualistic—things that made it difficult for my dad to comprehend. But even he couldn't deny how beautifully Jason rode.

"It's pretty good, not too shabby," Dad slurred. "Miss Ryan, your turn."

Instead of flipping him off, which was the knee-jerk reaction that popped into my head, I pedaled hard at the ramp, popped off the coping, and swung my back end like a machete to crank a turndown. I landed low and nearly clipped Dad's Bronco with my handlebars on the way back.

"It comes out of your ass if you scratch my truck." Dad was a difficult person to reason with when he was sober. Drunk, he operated with the logic of a rabid animal. He grabbed a beer from his mini fridge, then said, "You boys having fun with those high school girls yet, or what?" Jason and I awkwardly forced a laugh and glanced at each other.

"What, you're not fairies, are you?"

Seething, I clenched my jaw. Jason and I exchanged another quick glance. Not for the first time, I wondered if my dad somehow knew what we did when we were alone.

"Don't get pissy, Ry," he said. "You can't be so sensitive." He cracked a Milwaukee's Best, took a swig, then said, "All I can tell you is, get as much as you can while you're young." He stood on unsteady feet, looking at me like he was laying down some profound wisdom.

Not sure what else to do, Jason and I hit the quarter pipe a few more times. Dad eventually said, "I guess I'll leave you girls to it, even though it is *my shop*." He slammed the door on his way out like an oaf.

After he left, I sat on my bike, silenced by embarrassment. Jason knew my dad drank a lot, but he'd never seen him in this state of belligerence. Instead of telling me everything would be okay or some other bullshit, he said, "Sounds like he's got a ferret in his ass," mocking Dad's slurred speech. We died laughing.

21

With snow on the ground, Jason and I met up with Devin pretty much every weekend to ride the indoor ramps at Incline, PennSkate, or the Little Devil warehouse in Philly. I learned threes and started roasting them off box jumps and spines, and Jason learned three-sixty turndowns and started going even higher. When you watched him ride, you knew you were witnessing something inimitable and uncanny, like when you see a famous painting in person, and it has an aura photos can't capture.

We both started getting more attention in the BMX world. Jason got a double-page spread in *Ride*, blasting an invert off the wall at the Little Devil warehouse; and I got a quarter-page photo in *Faction*, a respected but lesser-known magazine, doing a turndown over the spine at Incline. Devin told the owner of FBM about Jason and showed him some footage. Jason and Frank had a short phone call, and, easy as that, a frame and box of parts arrived at Jason's house. He was on the flow team.

I looked over his brand-new Night Train frame, running my hand along the top tube, then said, "You're not going to become one of those FBM dudes who just parties and doesn't ride, are you?"

"Widdle baby's jealous?"

I told him to go fuck himself. He asked me if I wanted his Terrible One frame, rubbing salt in the wound.

My jealousy was regrettable, especially since I was getting recognition most kids our age coveted. The owner of Little Devil gave both of us any shirts or hoodies we wanted. When *Criminal Mischief* came out, people started recognizing us from our clips in the friends section.

In our secret life, we progressed from using our hands to using our mouths. You might be surprised by how many well-known riders were part of that scene. Or maybe you wouldn't. Guys would typically make little jokes or veiled comments if they knew about it. I had recently discovered books like *Junkie* and *The Basketball Diaries*. Reading about the underworld people inhabited when addicted to heroin reminded me of this side of BMX. You could tell with a wink who knew and who didn't.

Internet porn was still novel, and I remember feeling queasy the first time I watched a guy give another guy head. I came almost immediately—and obsessively made sure I erased the browser history since I was using our family computer. I still looked at women, but I liked how when guys did stuff together, you could tell there was insider expertise. The guilt and anxiety never went away, though, and it was always sharpest after Jason and I fooled around alone. There was something warm and caring in the way we touched each other, which added another layer of confusion I didn't know how to parse. All the while, I was waking up in the middle of the night, my chest tight, after dreams about our excursions at Chunk House. I would see flashes of us in a circle, surrounding the grimy towel. The thick male stench would hit me all over again.

∽

Devin brought Josh Stricker up to Suffield to ride with us in January. So there we were, watching two of our favorite riders shred a quarter pipe we'd built in my dad's workshop. Stricker rode with such urgency, like every run might be his last. Watching his video parts, you might think he only rode like that for the camera, but that was just his style. "This ramp is sick," he said after a run. He wiped sweat from his brow and flipped his hair out of his eyes. Coming from him, the small compliment meant the world to us. But Jason and I made sure to play it cool and not nerd out.

Devin rode with a more casual vibe, boosting stylish airs almost as an afterthought and doing wall taps a few inches above Jason's highest marks. While we took a break between runs, Devin told us about meeting a fifteen-year-old girl at a skatepark, renting a hotel room, and fucking her in the hot tub.

I introduced Devin and Stricker to my parents after our session. Mom said, "Thanks for watching out for the boys. They really look up to you guys."

"Oh, I'm happy to, Mrs. Thompson," Devin said, sounding snottier than Eddie Haskell and grinning. "They're such sweet boys."

"Aren't you a little old to be hanging out with teenagers?" Dad asked. He was never one to mince words.

Devin was caught off guard. "It's hard to find dudes as good as them," he fumbled.

Dad stared at him. I wondered why he couldn't turn off his impulse to be a dick for just one night. When Dad couldn't see, I looked at Devin and rolled my eyes.

At school, Jason and I had one foot in and one foot out more than ever. We already had an us versus them mentality before everything with Tanner went down. After that, the distance between us and everyone at school was as obvious as a face tattoo. We talked shit to people constantly, oftentimes without them realizing, which was a tactic we'd learned from Devin. We wore Dickies, trucker hats, and shirts with brands our classmates would never recognize. We'd both grown out our hair so it covered our ears. My dad told me I looked like a girl even though his hair was longer than mine in the seventies. Jason's black hair was perfectly straight. Set against his pale skin, his long hair made him look a bit like Danzig, just without the muscles. We might as well have been living on a different planet than our classmates.

Captain Kurt stopped Jason in the hall after lunch one day and said, "You little queers really think you're better than us, don't you."

Jason just said, "Yes," and kept walking.

22

Our main goal the summer before our senior year was to make our trails gnarlier, with the unspoken sub-goal of making them bigger than anything at Posh or Catty. Once again, all our lips and landings got steeper. The jumps pitched you straight up into the air and made you feel like you'd never come down.

We also started digging at Posh when we drove down to Bethlehem. Watching Devin, Neb, and Trevor build, it was clear that we were watching artists whose medium was dirt, whose paint brushes were shovels. Each of their movements had a clear purpose and intent. They had different spots where they'd get dirt for the foundation of a jump and where they'd get the more clay-heavy soil for the top layers. They'd get a shovelful and fling it at a specific area with the precision of expert fly fishermen.

We'd shown Devin footage and pictures of our trails, but he didn't ride them until that summer, when he brought up a filmer who was working on the Manmade video. When the guy saw Orion, he just said, "What the fuck?"

Jason and I rode like usual, and the guy filmed. Wanting footage for his section, Devin tried to three the first jump of Orion, but he over-rotated, landed low, and his left foot slipped off his pedal. He bailed, ghosting his bike off the next lip. To be a smartass, I three-sixtied the same jump my next run, gliding into the landing and roasting the rest of the line. Devin accepted that Jason had surpassed him as a rider, but he hated when I showed him up—and it was happening more often.

I was sitting on my bike and resting at the top when he snuck up behind me and put me in a tight headlock. I kicked my bike away and tried to fight him off, but Devin had a hundred pounds over me, easy, and he was taller by a few inches. Laughing in my ear, he said, "Say Daddy Devin has a big dick." His voice rose in pitch like he was talking to a child. Jason and the filmer watched and laughed.

"Get the fuck off me. I'll kill you," I choked out as he squeezed my neck tighter, constricting my airway. I looked Jason in the eyes while he laughed, wondering why he wasn't helping me. When Devin finally let me go, I saw a flathead shovel and wanted very badly to hit him with it. The look on my face must've said as much.

"I'm just messing with you, Ry," he said. "Don't be a pussy."

This was part of the culture of constantly fucking with each other: you had to take it when it happened to you and laugh it off. If you couldn't do that, you were soft—and you should probably find someone else to hang out with. I caught my breath and picked up my bike, trying not to let my anger and fear show. I felt powerless in Devin's arms, like he could do anything he wanted. That feeling was like trying to shove my fist in my mouth. For the rest of the session, I focused my energy on going higher and faster than him.

Devin and the filmer stayed with us at my parent's house. Around Mom and Dad, Devin kept up his sarcastically well-mannered routine, laying the compliments on thick and doing the dishes after Mom cooked meatloaf for us. Dad still didn't hide his dislike for him, looking at Devin like you would a gallon jug of piss on the side of the highway. By the end of the second day of filming, Jason and I had gathered enough footage on our jumps and ramps, along with clips we'd collected on our own, to comprise a split part, which came out the following year.

The Manmade video was the first time a lot of people really saw what Jason and I—Jason especially—could do. Everyone was mesmerized by his riding. There's a pretty even split of clips, but watching Jason ride, it was easy to forget everything I did. He not only did his tricks more stylishly and went higher than virtually everyone (next to Mike Aitken and Chase Hawk), but he did most of them with these quick, razor-sharp snaps, like a switchblade making a surprise appearance in a bar fight. Part of me wished I was the one who became the new hot little shit in the BMX world. I also knew it was inevitable that people would start worshipping Jason as a rider.

I can't tell you how many times I've watched our part over the years. The Manmade guys let us choose the song (with veto power if we chose some bullshit), and I think they were pleasantly surprised when we picked At the Drive-In's "Arcarsenal." High-energy post-punk with sharp transitions between quiet and loud, it was our emotional lives in music. Our part usually makes me glow and feel deeply sad at the same time. Whether we're riding our trails or the ramp in Dad's shop, you can see so clearly on our faces that nothing else mattered. Life outside of riding spilled over at the edges, but it ceased to exist for those brief seconds when we were floating.

Me airing the first jump of Orion

23

"Fuck yeah, Ry," Jason said as I landed back in the quarter pipe after doing a wall tap high enough to graze my shoulder on the roof of the shop, which sprinkled dust in the air. Neither of us had to work that day, so we came home to ride right after school.

It was early March of our senior year, and Suffield was still under two feet of snow. Our classmates constantly talked about what colleges they'd applied to, about all the amazing things they planned to do once they got into the school of their dreams. I'd taken the SATs the previous spring and gotten accepted into Temple in Philly as an early applicant, but I still hadn't told Jason. He didn't apply to college. There was no way Laurie could afford it. Having half-assed our way through high school, neither of us were competitive for any scholarships. Riding our ramp that afternoon, I blurted out that I was going to Temple.

Jason forced a smile and said, "That's awesome." He and I both knew this would happen, but the sudden reality of it was sandpaper on skin. He spun his pedals backward one rotation, sat on his bike, and cleared his throat. "I've actually been talking with a few guys from Bethlehem about renting a house near Posh." He hadn't said anything about it to me until that moment, so I felt somewhat betrayed.

"Hell yeah," I said. "We'll be able to ride together all the time." The short distance between Bethlehem and Philly was a salve, but it was clear that change had been set in motion. I wouldn't have admitted that I was scared to move away, especially since I'd been talking shit about Suffield since middle school—but I was. While I obviously couldn't wait to get out of my dad's house, I wanted everything between Jason and me to stay the same.

As Jason rode that afternoon, the sounds of wood slapping concrete and the coping getting jostled rose above the din of Converge's metallic hardcore playing on Dad's stereo. Jason had gotten to the point where he had to moderate his airs in the shop, which had a twelve-foot-roof, so he didn't hit his head. Gravity didn't seem to exist in the same way for him.

We rode for forty or so minutes but then started feeling restless. My parents weren't due home for at least another hour, so we decided to go into the enclosed tool room, which had become our place to fool around when it was too cold to ride outside. Neither Jason nor I even thought about watching out for my parents. There was something more pressing to deal with.

Of course my dad came home early, and of course we didn't hear him yell our names over the loud music. We were focused on how good we were starting to feel—on the mad rush of blood that tunneled our reality, and the sharp need to extract that energy.

And, of course, he caught us.

When my dad opened the tool room door, he made a disgusted sound, like he'd witnessed a botched surgery. The horrified look on his face is burned into my memory. "Are you fucking kidding me? What's wrong with you? Get the hell out of my tool room." His voice resounded in my body. Not wanting to see more, he turned around without shutting the door.

We hurriedly pulled up our pants. Jason grabbed his bike without saying a word or looking at Dad and left. The Cutlass's tires crunched on gravel, and the exhaust gargled as he drove away.

I desperately wished I was with him. I'd only ever seen such white-hot anger in Dad's eyes one other time in my life, when some frat guys in New Haven said something about Mom's ass after a movie.

"How could you do this to me? Everyone in this town knows who I am." He kept yelling inane shit like this.

As ignorance spewed from his mouth, my body responded before my brain could stop it, years of molten anger finally erupting. I punched my dad as hard as I could in the jaw, even though he was much bigger than me. I wish I could forget it: the dull thud of knuckle on bone and the immediate jolt of pain that shot through my arm after my fist connected.

Dad was stunned.

It was pure instinct when he punched me back, giving me what would become the worst black eye of my life and knocking me to the ground. Waking up the next morning, I felt like I'd gotten hit by a Mack truck. My head throbbed for the better part of two days. For Dad's hand, my face was clay.

"That didn't need to happen, Ry." His voice was ragged. "Why the fuck did you make me do that?"

I was still on the ground, dazed and covering my face.

He took a few steps backward, then turned around and walked outside, tromping through snow. I heard the back door of the house slam shut.

Mom eventually came home, pulling into the driveway like any other day. I made sure to turn off the stereo before I walked out to face whatever was going to happen next.

PART TWO

Stress Fractures

24

As I walked past old stone buildings on my first day of class, I remember thinking, *How the fuck did they let me in here?* Temple wasn't Harvard by any means, but I could immediately tell that skating by, like I had for my entire high school career, would no longer cut it. The kids in my classes were the types who never stopped trying to be smart, although you also had the obligatory meatheads and party people who, if they didn't flunk out, would barely make it through.

I got in because of my entrance essay, which I wrote about riding trails. Along with my grades, my SAT scores were nothing special. But I actually tried with the essay. I knew a lot of people would send in the typical five-paragraph bullshit, so I dove into these little ruminations about connecting with nature through BMX and finding beauty in something most people overlook or dismiss. Instead of evidence of extracurriculars, I sent in a few photos of our jumps and some magazine pictures of mine and Jason's.

My roommate in the dorms was this nerdy kid named Harold, a good Catholic boy. He had black-framed glasses, neatly combed brown hair, and a doughy face. He was not what you would call pleased when I hung up my Eyehategod poster, which Jason had bought me for this specific purpose: to troll my roommate. It also reminded me of him. Eager to get out of Suffield, Jason had gone through with his plan to move into a house in Bethlehem with a few of the Posh guys.

I got a job at a crappy pizza place near campus where I was supposed to do everything from cooking and working the register to cleaning. I ended up being primarily a dishwasher because I sucked at interacting with the public if I didn't want to, plus most of the people who frequented the place were bro types. Sometimes the owner would walk by me while I was washing dishes and say, "Let's go, Ryan!" in a deep, pump-up-your-teammate voice and hold up his hand for me to slap.

Any extra time I had, I drove the hour up to Posh to dig and ride.

Aside from living in a new place and not having as much time on my hands because I actually had to study (flunking out and pissing away Dad's money wasn't an option), it felt in some ways like things hadn't changed a whole lot. I lived within riding distance of the Little Devil warehouse, and Jason and I started meeting up with Van Homan at FDR, this gnarly DIY concrete park some skaters had built in the early nineties. I loved pedaling through Philly. If it was warm, people were out living their lives, doing whatever they did. The city had a hum to it, a music. Suffield was always dead quiet.

Jason and I rode Catty and Posh early on Sunday mornings, when we were the only ones there. Every time I rode either set of trails, I was continually blown away by how well everything fit together. All the lines flowed and interconnected in perfect synchronicity with the land, with each rise and dip in the ground. The paths for each line were worn so smooth, it seemed like they'd always been there. I loved Philadelphia, but living in a crowded city for the first time could also get overwhelming. Everything from going to the store to parking required more effort. Riding in the woods, I was able to wipe the slate clean.

Jason went pro for FBM, which was no surprise. Williamson gave him another new frame and started sending him $300 checks every month. To have his expenses covered, Jason only had to work a few days a week as a helper at a machine shop. Standard, a respected core company, started flowing me frames and parts. They supported riders who flew under the radar, and the owner didn't care whether I competed or not. He wanted me to keep getting coverage like I already was, but even that didn't seem to matter that much to him. Standard and similar companies often gave products to people whose riding fit their brand aesthetic. It helped that I rode and dug at Posh. Having a trail rat support the company at one of the most iconic spots in the world reinforced Standard's reputation as being genuinely dedicated to BMX. As cool as it was to get free frames and parts, I never actually got paid for riding.

I obviously coveted what Jason had, but I think the feeling went both ways. Going pro had been a goal of ours since middle school. Jason was one of the chosen few who made that dream a reality. I still told myself I could get there if I started going faster and higher, if I pushed harder and let go of my fear more. Really, I knew my skill would always be a blip on the radar compared to Jason's explosive talent. What I didn't think about much back then was how Jason wished he could've gone to college. When he got his first check from FBM and showed it to me, envy must've been written on my forehead. "This is chump change compared to what you'll make with your sophisticated education," Jason said, enunciating the last part like an Ivy League asshole. We both knew it was true. Still, if I had the choice, I would've traded my education and privilege for his ability in a heartbeat.

Jason, table at Catty

Mom and Dad's divorce was still raw when I started at Temple. I was grateful to finally be out of the house. I couldn't help but fall into the predictable trap of blaming myself for their breakup—and that feeling wouldn't let up when I was at home. Really, they'd grown apart long before Dad punched me in the shop. They were two mismatched puzzle pieces who'd been trying to force themselves together for over twenty years. Part of me was relieved that the pressure valve had finally been released because I think they would've hung on indefinitely if Dad hadn't given me a black eye. When Mom looked at him after that, there was no love—not even a glimmer. She'd dealt with multiple students over the years who were getting abused at home, so it was a black-and-white decision for her, even though I told her several times that I threw the first punch.

She separated from Dad three weeks after the shop incident. There were several nights of him desperately (often drunkenly) begging Mom to give him another chance. But it didn't matter. Whatever was left of their foundation had finally eroded. Mom applied for a job teaching high school in New Haven but didn't tell us until she got it.

One evening during the summer, when she was in the process of moving out and all her stuff was packed neatly in brand-new cardboard boxes, Dad ordered takeout for us. Mom, Dad, and I sat in the dining room of what suddenly felt like a starkly empty house. I was getting ready to move out, too. Only a few bites into his chow mein, Dad broke down. "I wish I could take it back, Ry," he said for what seemed like the thousandth time. "I'm so sorry." As many times as he'd wanted to hit me over the years, I think the reality of it reminded him how small and ashamed he felt when Grandpa laid hands on him and his brother.

"I know, Dad. It was just a fucked-up situation."

Truth is, I did forgive him—for punching me, at least. He'd reacted exactly the way you'd expect a crusty steel worker's son to react. I can tell you with certainty that, if Grandpa had caught Dad doing something like that, he would've been the first *and* last one to swing. We had both purged some pent-up rage during the blowout. Without as much anger seething between us, however, we were left with a new space neither of us knew how to deal with.

I lived with Dad for another month and a half after Mom moved out because I didn't want to move twice with college right around the corner. When Jason came over in the immediate aftermath, he would glance at Dad, then keep his eyes on the ground. He stopped coming inside. Two or three weeks after Mom left, Jason and I drove to Rhode Island to check out some guys' jumps. He dropped me off at home when the sun was setting. As I unlatched my bike from the rack on the Cutlass, Dad opened the front door and shouted, "Let's hang out tonight, boys." Jason looked at me, shrugged, and then shut off his engine and took the keys out of the ignition.

The beer stench hit me like a wall as soon as I walked inside. Dad had always done his drinking in the shop, but he got plastered right in the living room most nights during that brief period when we lived alone together. Crushed cans were littered at the foot of his recliner. That's when you really knew Dad had tied one on: if he stopped throwing his cans away. He was otherwise a bit of a neat freak.

"Fuck it," Dad said. "Let's order pizza and watch a movie." Before we answered, he was on the phone, ordering three large pizzas from Domino's. I couldn't tell if he was growing a beard or had just stopped caring. He hung up and clumsily gestured at the fridge. "I bought some cheerleader beer for you girls." He'd gotten us a six-pack of Mike's Hard Lemonade. I guess he thought getting drunk together would be a bonding experience. Afraid to lose his son in addition to his wife, he was grasping at straws.

Not knowing what else to do, Jason and I got buzzed with him, ate pizza, and watched *The Goonies*. Dad was in and out, laughing at the parts with Chunk and Sloth but not reacting to much else. He passed out a little over halfway through and started snoring. Jason at least waited until the end of the movie before he got up and left.

So yeah, those last weeks of living at home were awkward, stilted. Everything felt precarious. Dad and I needed time on our own to figure things out. College came around at the perfect moment.

The next time I hung out with Jason, I said, "My dad can be such a caveman. Just a total moron."

"He still loves us, Ry."

"He punched me in the face. And all the homophobic shit is completely fucked."

"He's from a different generation…and you swung first." I was quiet, stewing. Jason said, "I'm just trying to say you should feel lucky to have a dad." It knocked the wind out of me.

Jason and I began doing what we did alone more often and with more abandon after the shop incident. In a way, getting caught by Dad eased some of my stress. Now, I didn't obsessively worry about what would happen if my parents found out. I think my mom knew earlier but didn't want to say anything and make me feel ashamed. Afterward, she said, "You have to try things to find out what you like. It's totally normal." (I don't know if Jason ever told his mom about my dad catching us in the tool room.) But I'd still get lost in that familiar haze of anxiety, repeatedly questioning if I was straight or gay, with neither label feeling right. The nightmares of us standing around the dirty towel at Chunk House never stopped. I'd see flashes of Devin's bearded face and yell out, waking myself up.

∿

Jason came down to Philly on a Thursday evening not long after school started. We had a session at the Little Devil ramps, then pedaled back to my dorm room. Those dudes bought us a couple forties, so Jason and I got nice and loose.

Harold was lying in bed, trying to read an Isaac Asimov novel. He was not happy about us drinking in the dorms, even though people on our floor partied constantly. He kept clearing his throat and glaring at us over his glasses, which we thought was hilarious.

"Harry," Jason said with a ghoulish smile. He held out his forty to Harold. "Try this Olde E. It tastes better than pirate cum."

"Yeah, Harry," I said in a crusty pirate voice. "Gargle ye jizz and we can listen to Eyehategod."

Jason started rubbing me through my jeans. "Hey, Harry," he said, "you ever get jacked off by one of your friends?" He was genuinely inviting him to join, but it obviously wasn't without malice.

I'd felt angry and embarrassed when Jason fucked with Tanner like this in high school. Those feelings bubbled up again, but I laughed like a fiend at the absolute horror on Harold's face. He covered his head with his pillow, probably wondering what godless pit his roommate had crawled out of. In our closet-sized room, there was no escape.

Guilt congealed in my intestines when Jason left the next morning. Harold wouldn't look at or speak to me. I knew that feeling: that confusion about when joking around becomes something darker, and the sudden realization that you have little to no idea what people do behind closed doors.

25

This dorky dude named Mitch started coming to Posh and Catty. Everyone let him ride because Devin liked fucking with him so much. He wore a full-face helmet and Xtra Skins shin guards; he had a gross goatee that he dyed green; and, at the ripe age of twenty-one, he had his ex-wife's name tattooed on his neck. It was faded and barely legible, looking like the artist's first attempt at cursive. Mitch could make it through the jumps, but then he'd do these ridiculous no-footers and one-handers over the last sets and yell "Yeah!" to himself.

Devin would shout, "Fuck yeah, Misty! That one made me hard as a rock," and we'd all double over laughing.

Using people as human props was obviously nothing new to us. In one of our favorite videos, Uproot's *Laid to Waste*, the riders got a homeless man, Snake, who had severe mental illness, to do the intros for each rider. He wore a puffy Falcons jacket, his thin hair was disheveled, and he had glasses with large brown frames. Holding an old revolver, his hand wavered from side to side as he said, "I'll shoot you in your crazy hair, Greg Wilcox." The gun the riders let Snake use was real. In another intro, he mumbled, "Here's a dinosaur bone, and this is Ben Harris," as he shakily held a large dog bone. Sounding like he was talking to a house pet, the rider behind the camera immediately ordered Snake to "do it again." After introducing a later section, Snake ate half a stick of margarine, nodded, and said, "Pretty good." You could see in his blank gaze how unwell he was. We were friends with the Uproot guys. I could tell you that this humor didn't sit right with me—but there I was, not stopping it and, more often than not, laughing along.

In addition to Mitch, there was this hessian kid with shoulder-length hair named Joe who Devin met somewhere and started bringing to parties. I think the kid used to ride in some capacity because he knew most of us by name, even though we'd never seen him before. He only came over to Chunk House a handful of times, and he was tripping on acid each time. Everyone would crowd around him and dart around like ghosts to fuck with his head. I can only imagine what the kid saw. The look on his face was sheer terror.

But Mitch got it the worst, by far.

26

If you tried to ride FDR when skaters were at the park, they'd beat your ass if you were alone or start a fight if you were in a group. You had to ride it early in the morning if you didn't want to deal with that bullshit.

Our Sunday morning sessions there and at Posh and Catty are stored in some holy space in my brain. I loved waking up early and, without having time to think about the outside world, packing up and heading out to ride. It didn't give my stress a chance to take hold.

Watching Van Homan flow at FDR was like watching a really good drummer flow on the drums—when all the different grooves, rhythms, and fills blur together as the person chases each one to unexpected conclusions. He blasted the hips and carved the bowls with such force that I half-expected to see divots in the concrete after his runs. This was when I realized that riding concrete skateparks could occupy a similar aesthetic realm as riding trails. In my mind, though, trails were always and forever the purest form of BMX.

Jason started shredding FDR pretty much immediately. The skaters who built it had no intention of making it accessible to beginners. All the quarter pipes were steep with jutting coping, and the feel of the transitions could be radically different from one to the next. Jason would blast them in a way that made you think he was never coming down. He'd do these gorgeous lip-slide bonks on the over-vert part of the bowl corner, tapping his tire on the edge with a delicate pugilism. Then he'd fly up the skinny vert walls like a bird of prey.

I loved those vert walls. Built on the legs of the bridge that covered the skatepark, you could shoot up them and feel suspended, hanging in the air as traffic droned above you. There's a Superman roller coaster in California that reminds me of those vert walls. You rocketed up the transition and gradually lost momentum to hang in this liminal space before gaining speed the other way and blazing back down.

During a session just before the real cold of winter arrived, Jason ran a line he'd been doing all fall. For him, it was tame. That's often how it went. Many of the worst wrecks I saw happened when people were doing things they'd done countless times before. You'd think the most brutal crashes would happen on the gnarly stuff people thought about for years before trying—but your awareness sharpened during those moments, so you often found a way to bail.

Jason waited on the deck of a quarter pipe while I finished a run, then he dropped in, did a lookback over a hip, ripped around the bowl corner, and shot up the main vert wall. On his way back down, his front wheel swerved off the side. He was loose and casual and didn't have time to shield his face. He hit the ground with a slap that makes me cringe to think about. Compared to the thunderclap of flesh and bone slamming into concrete, the metallic bounce of his bike was like a dinging bell.

I rushed over. He was dazed but awake. He looked at me as I held him in my arms, his eyes pointing in different directions for a split second. His mouth was a bloody mess, and his right thumb pointed the wrong way. I picked him up in a fireman's carry and set him in the passenger seat of my truck. I thought about leaving our bikes, but I knew they'd get stolen, so I threw them in the bed as fast as I could. Luckily, the nearest hospital wasn't too far away.

"You little assholes," Laurie said after she pushed past a nurse to get into Jason's room. "Let me guess, you weren't wearing your goddamn helmets."

Jason was soaring on pain meds, his thumb was badly broken but at least in the right place, and he was running his tongue over the little nubbin where his left-front tooth used to be. "It's okay, Mom," he said, smiling like a goon. "I've always wanted to be a pirate." I couldn't help myself from letting a laugh escape.

Laurie snapped around. "And what about you, Ryan? You think it's funny for me to get called at work and told that my son is mangled—and then have to drive four hours to fucking Pennsylvania, worried sick?"

She and Mom were the same that way. If they called you by your whole first name, you were in deep shit.

As always, she made us promise to start wearing helmets, and not just at indoor skateparks where we had to. Jason said, "Yeah, Mom, totally, of course, we gotta now, pretty much have to," at which, in my poor judgment, I laughed again.

Laurie cut through me with her glare. "I'm fucking serious this time, Ryan. You guys go too high and fast to fuck around with your brains. If you do it and tell him to, Jason will wear one."

I promised we would, although that was broken the next time I was on my bike, and same with Jason after he healed. All I can really tell you about not wearing helmets is that it was an aesthetic decision—a horribly stupid and ill-informed one, but an aesthetic decision nonetheless.

∿

With winter bearing down, everyone at Jason's house drank themselves stupid every night. When he got bored with that, Jason would come to the dorms and play *Pro Skater* with me and Harold, who was turning a new leaf. His hair was getting shaggy, and he'd asked me to teach him about Slayer. We got wasted on High Life and listened to *Reign In Blood* at least three times through, and then we did the same thing the next two nights. Harold began smoking cigarettes in our room, which I didn't mind because I've always liked the smell of secondhand smoke for some reason. He started calling his fellow computer science majors "little Pillsburies" because, he said, they were soft.

Jason tried to play despite the awkwardness of his cast, but he couldn't handle the controller. This one night, Harold was having none of it. "No, dipshit," he said, snatching the controller away. "You have to transfer from the *other* spine to find the hidden section."

Jason and I busted up laughing. "You know what, Harry?" Jason said, patting his shoulder. "You're all right, my friend." Harold loved this but knew enough by then not to let on.

27

I knew it was over for me when I saw her in that Converge sweatshirt, with her dark, chin-length hair, highlighted with red, and nose ring. Instead of gauged earrings, which were popular at the time, she had small silver hoops in both ears. She wore faded black Sevens and black Vans slip-ons. She had on a hint of eyeliner but hardly any makeup besides that. Petite with a subtle overbite, sly smile, and fierce eyes, she immediately struck me as one of the hottest girls I'd ever seen.

In the first critical theory course required for English majors, this guy Jonathan would answer every question in the most affected Ivy League style he could muster. In response to his response to some question the professor asked about deconstruction, Natalie said, "You're completely off." She proceeded to light his argument on fire and piss on the ashes. Jonathan squirmed in his seat, trying to find places to interject. But Natalie's critique was airtight.

That's when I knew it was doubly over for me.

I sat near her in the next class. She wore a zip hoodie beneath her jean jacket, which had a Creed patch above the left-front pocket.

"You don't actually like Creed, do you?" I asked.

She laughed. "They're one of the worst bands of all time, but people make the funniest faces when they see it."

We walked away from class together, talking about Converge. Snow covered the grass on campus. The walkways were shoveled and speckled with salt. People walked hurriedly to get out of the cold. Natalie kept glancing over at me. I met her eyes but hesitated. Her lightly freckled cheeks took on a red hue in the icy air. She tucked her hair behind her ears and put on her hood.

"I better get to biology," she said when we got to a turnoff. "I guess I'll see you in class next week?"

"Okay, cool, see you then." I walked ten feet, then turned around. "Hey, Natalie," I said, practically shouting. "Do you want to go to a movie or something some time?"

She smiled. "That sounds awesome. I didn't think you were going to ask."

∿

Natalie's dad, Mark, was from Japan. He moved with his parents to the US when he was a teenager. He became successful doing something adjacent to venture capitalism, although Natalie thought it was a greedy, cut-throat profession. She tried explaining it to me, but I had no real idea what he did. Her mom, a white woman named Terry, had grown up in the suburbs of Chicago and was now a curator at ICA Boston. Natalie introduced me to them within a month. Hanging out after class in her dorm room one afternoon, she offhandedly said, "Oh yeah, we're eating dinner with my parents tonight." I was nervous, but I wanted to be with Natalie as often as I could, so I went along with it.

I could tell Terry liked me right away. She smiled when I talked and actually seemed interested in what I had to say. Her light brown hair was cropped short, and she wore a smart gray dress. Mark was harder to read. Wearing a black blazer and immaculately pressed white button-down, he looked at me like I was a newly discovered fungus he didn't know what to make of. His hair was slicked back, not one strand out of place.

Natalie had told me to bring some magazines with photos of me and Jason riding. I thought it was a ridiculous idea, especially as I walked into this upscale restaurant in downtown Philadelphia carrying BMX magazines. I've always hated dressing up, so I was wearing old jeans and a Little Devil shirt, plus my hair was looking pretty ratty. The hostess made a face like she'd stepped in poop when she saw me. I ordered a burger and then felt like a dumbass for it when Mark and Terry ordered bouillabaisse, and Natalie ordered filet mignon.

While we waited, Natalie said, "Dad, check out these pictures of Ryan and his friend riding jumps on their bikes."

I handed Mark the magazines, and he thumbed through them. I showed him a photo of Jason riding Posh in *DIG*, and one of me at Catty that *Ride* had recently published.

"I used to skateboard down some pretty steep hills in my previous life," he said. "But nothing this intense. How do you push past the fear?"

I fumbled for an answer, then finally said, "You can't think about it too much."

As we ate, I talked more about BMX, trying and failing to explain the transcendental experience that riding and building trails provided.

∿

I was more nervous for Natalie to meet Jason than my parents. I hadn't told her about what we did together yet. I worried she'd break up with me if I told her I was bisexual. I thought about how disgusted Christina had been.

On the other hand, I was afraid Jason would pull a Devin and mock everything she said. When I told him I was dating a girl, he sneered and said, "You didn't learn your lesson with Christina?" It was an asshole response, but I tried to brush it off.

Natalie and I met up with Jason in the courtyard below my dorm room. Dirty, hardened snowdrifts lined the walkways. "Natalie grew up going to hardcore shows in Boston," I blurted, not a minute after I introduced them. "She's seen Converge and Snapcase and a ton of others."

"Fuck yeah," Jason said. He blew into his hands and stuffed them in his sweatshirt pockets. "Did you ever run into any of those straight-edge gangs that beat the fuck out of drunk people at shows?"

Natalie laughed. "Oh my God," she said, "my dumbass ex-boyfriend was into that shit." On our way to the coffee shop, I could barely get a word in edgewise.

∿

The next time I hung out at Chunk House was later that spring. As I got drunk, laughed at Devin doing an impression of Mitch, and took hits from a joint, I decided it wouldn't be a big deal if I went into one of the rooms, watched what unfolded between the riders, and got myself off. What Natalie and I did together felt so much different than the things that happened at Chunk House. Plus, I was wasted. There was always a shift at the house when we were about to go into one of the back rooms. You could almost smell the need in the air, almost taste it.

I woke up early to Jason's loud snoring. I'd fallen asleep on a grimy couch. He and a few other riders were spread out on the filthy, once-tan carpet, sleeping with their heads on their arms. I felt sick with dread.

That afternoon, I anxiously told Natalie everything as we sat on her bed in her dorm room. Unlike me and Harold, Natalie and her roommate actually cleaned up after themselves. Their room smelled of the lemon-scented lotion Natalie used. A framed Le Tigre poster hung on the wall next to her bed. In front of a pink backdrop, Kathleen Hanna and Johanna Fateman stood behind JD Samson. With her wispy mustache and tuxedo, Samson looked like she was daring you to fuck with her.

"I wish we would've talked about this before you went over there," Natalie said. She sat cross-legged, looking me in the eye as she spoke. She was disappointed and hurt, but she could tell how guilty I felt for messing around with dudes. I'd been reading Myspace posts about bi guys whose girlfriends broke up with them once they found out about their past, entries describing the common tendency for people to assume that if you liked fucking around with other guys at all, you had to be gay.

"The stuff at Chunk House is just part of the trail scene," I said. "It doesn't mean anything." My breath became tight as I told her about doing stuff with Jason when we were alone, and how I was still attracted to him. "But there's no question about my feelings for you. I'm honestly kind of scared by how intense they are." I looked down at the vacuumed carpet.

"Sexuality is a spectrum," Natalie said after a moment. "I have no idea how anyone got it in their heads that most people fall neatly into one category. But I need to be the only person you're with. I don't want to be in an open relationship."

She grabbed the collar of my shirt, pulled me to her, and kissed me. That was the first time I thought, *I want to marry this person.* Aside from Jason and the riders we fooled around with, she was the only person who told me it was okay to feel the things I did, to have done the things I had. Natalie was outside our world, so her words were more affirming. I felt seen and accepted by her, like I didn't have to hide.

As I told her that, as long as we were together, I wouldn't screw around with Jason or anyone else, my stomach sank. I didn't know if it was a promise I could keep. Natalie knew it wouldn't be right to ask me to stop being friends with Jason, but I began to notice a wariness on her face when I'd leave to hang out with him.

∿

Jason and I were in my dorm room alone a week later, listening to Cavity and drinking High Life. We sat on the crumb-speckled floor, our backs against my bed. He started rubbing my jeans. I got up to get another beer, but he grabbed my wrist and pulled me toward him. He was taken aback when I yanked my arm away.

"I love Natalie," I blurted, which was true. I just hadn't told her yet.

Jason put his hand back in his lap. His face turned red, but he forced a smile. "I totally get it, man." He looked at the floor. "She's rad."

I could feel something new and unfamiliar opening between us. It was wrenching. But I was falling so hard for Natalie, and I didn't want to fuck that up.

I grabbed a beer from the mini fridge and sat back down, not knowing what to say. Jason put his face in his hands for a second and then looked at me. "I love you, Ry."

"I love you, too."

"No. I'm in love with you."

I didn't know how to respond—we'd never said those words to each other—so I awkwardly stared at Harold's *Predator* poster hanging crookedly behind the TV. I had somehow blocked off the thought, so it hadn't surfaced. All of a sudden, there it was: I was in love with Jason, too. I had the distinct sensation that someone was trying to cleave my chest in two. I kept staring at Schwarzenegger's empty eyes and bulging arms, not saying anything.

Wanting to drown the sudden awkwardness between us, we got hammered and decided to go to one of the bro's rooms to see if we could find someone with weed. We did, and we got very twisted. Suddenly, there were two of everything. Their room smelled like ass and bong water. Dirty clothes blanketed the floor. Jason kept yelling "I *love* Dave Mathews Band" to the patchouli bros and pumping his fist in the air.

I ended up puking my guts out in the communal bathroom. Some guy who was brushing his teeth overheard me and said, "Fuck yeah, baby. I get hard when you throw up like that."

"Eat a dick, you fucking Chad moron," Jason shot back.

"Easy, sister," the guy said. "I was just kidding around."

Jason patted my back as I vomited, and, when I was done, helped me back to my room, flopping me onto the bed. I took off my shirt, about to pass out.

"I think I'll just drive back to Bethlehem," Jason said. I was more wasted than him, but he teetered on his feet.

"Fuck you. Give me your keys," I slurred. I slumped on my bed, struggling to keep my eyes open.

"Just go to sleep, dumbass. I'll be fine."

In my head, I tried to stop him, but it was likely just a feeble attempt to grab his arm. I closed my eyes…and woke up to gray morning light seeping through the dusty blinds. I frantically called Jason every ten minutes for the next three hours until he picked up. I tried to distract myself by watching episodes of *Curb Your Enthusiasm*, but it didn't work.

"What's up, darling?" he said when he finally answered. "You worried about your little pirate?"

"Dude, don't drive like that. I'm serious. It's stupid as fuck."

"You don't have to worry about me, baby. I'm a big boy. I can wipe my own ass and everything." Him trying to joke his way out of it made me want to punch a wall. Before he answered his phone, I kept seeing flashes of his lifeless body on the highway, blood pouring from his head onto the salted concrete.

28

"Who were your favorite authors when you were a kid?" Natalie asked. We'd hung out all day but still felt the need to talk on the phone that night, not wanting to miss an instant of each other's life.

"Um…I remember liking Dr. Seuss a lot when I was little. It's cool how he was able to pack an environmentalist message into *The Lorax*." Irritated that I was on the phone again, Harold turned around from his desk, looked at me, and then shook his head while putting on a big pair of headphones.

"You know he was super racist, right?" Natalie said.

"Who? The Lorax?"

"No, dude. Dr. Seuss."

"No way. Dr. Seuss?"

"Before he got famous for doing kids' books, he used to do these political cartoons with disgusting caricatures of Japanese people."

I still didn't believe her, so, the next day, I went to the campus library and found exactly what she was talking about in an old volume of political cartoons from the WWII era. I was stunned in the way a white boy from a small town in Connecticut could be stunned by such things, which is to say I'd glimpsed beyond my curtain of privilege and was disturbed by what I saw. I felt like an idiot for not discovering it on my own.

Not long after, I was browsing the magazine rack near the register in the bookstore where Natalie worked, waiting for her to finish her shift. Her parents had repeatedly told her she didn't need to get a job. They preferred that she focus on school. She'd grown up around horribly spoiled rich kids, the vast majority of whom were deeply proud of the fact that earning a living for themselves was an option rather than a necessity, even though they had nothing to do with how their family had amassed money. Natalie didn't want to be one of them, which was partly why, to her parents' dismay, she chose Temple instead of UPenn or Cornell, where she'd also gotten accepted. "I didn't want to go to college with a bunch of rich assholes," she told me. "That's all it was at my high school."

I was skimming an issue of *Thrasher* when I heard her say, "Wouldn't you rather read a book that's actually written by a Japanese person?" She picked up the copy of *Memoirs of a Geisha* a couple was trying to buy, looking at it like a booger.

"Excuse me?" the woman said. It was a white suburban couple who were on an adventure in the city. They wore matching Columbia ski jackets and brand-new jeans. Offended, the woman opened her mouth in disbelief and put her hand on her chest.

"It's just, I'm sure you could find something better by a Japanese writer instead of a white guy writing about that culture." Natalie looked at the woman, unwavering.

The man stepped in front of his wife as if shielding her from a bullet. The look on their faces was hilarious until they started demanding to see the manager. I hung off to the side, not sure if I should get involved.

Natalie went to the back and got her boss, Alex, who apologized profusely and gave the couple the book on the house to keep the peace. After they left, Alex told Natalie not to let it happen again, but he let her off easy.

We were lying in her bed two or three nights earlier when she said, not for the first time, "I can't believe *Memoirs of a Geisha* is still so huge. The number of people who come in and buy that book is out of hand."

Walking away from the bookstore after her encounter with the suburban couple, I remember thinking that was one of the reasons I was falling so hard for her: she's one of those rare people for whom thought and action go hand in hand. I was enjoying the process of discovering challenging new ideas in college, but there was also a point where the abstractions and jargon seemed too disconnected from the world. BMX had its own specialized vocabulary, but it all referred to concrete physical movements. Academic jargon built abstract definitions atop abstract definitions, quickly creating a language void.

At the same time, I was becoming more aware of the limitations of BMX and its culture. So much of it was about turning off the nag of consciousness and obeying your body. But that was its own dead end. When I tried to talk to Jason and other riders about what I was reading, their eyes would glaze over, or they would look at each other and roll their eyes. I was becoming curious about what made society tick and how I could fit into it without becoming another capitalist asshole—but people didn't go to Posh to have discussions about social ills.

Natalie loved delving into the minutiae of different theoretical and literary concepts, but she kept her feet planted in the dirt of reality. She acted on her ideas instead of surrounding them with unnecessary layers of abstraction, which is what a lot of scholars seemed to do. That said, I sometimes felt like I couldn't let go around her, like I always had to be deep and thoughtful. I liked talking about serious shit, but I also liked laughing at dick jokes.

Jackass: The Movie came out a couple weeks after Jason told me he was in love with me. When I asked Natalie if she wanted to go, she said, "You're not serious, are you?"

"Yeah, let's go," I said. "It's idiotic, but it will be hilarious."

"Those assholes fuck with animals way too much," she said. "It's all frat boy humor. I thought you hated fraternity guys."

I had planned on telling Natalie about my and Jason's *Jackass* video stunts from high school. Now, I was embarrassed to bring it up. I thought about asking Jason to go to the movie but didn't know if it would be awkward to hang out on our own if we weren't riding. I went alone and laughed hysterically the entire time, although I wished Jason was with me. My stomach was sore for a full day afterward.

29

The summer after freshman year was the first in a long time when Jason and I didn't spend every free moment together. We still dug and rode together at Posh, but as holy as that place was, I realized they would always be someone else's jumps. The reward of building there wasn't the same as at our own trails. Not wanting to spend another year in the dorms, Harold and I moved into an apartment together near campus. Living with my dad in Suffield for the summer wasn't an option as far as I was concerned.

I hung out with Natalie a lot more, not spending nearly as much time on my bike. She and her friend had also started renting a place close to Temple. I could clearly picture the irritated look on Jason's face when he'd call and ask me if I wanted to ride, and I would tell him I already had plans. He started partying more. When we were together, his declaration loomed above us. Neither of us knew what to do with it. Did I need to tell him I felt the same way but was also deeply in love with Natalie? Or would that just amplify the tension between us? Should I tell him he should try dating other guys? Instead of diving into that quagmire, we stuck to what we knew: BMX.

Jason and I had both hopped on the Mike Aitken train and bought a few pairs of girl jeans. But when I went up to Bethlehem for a session at Catty, Jason was wearing skin-tight black Wranglers, which, I realized immediately, looked much more badass. Most of my professors were super square. They'd talk about anti-capitalist politics while wearing the most yuppie clothes imaginable: button-down shirts and khakis that made them look like they'd stepped out of a Dockers ad. I'd heard multiple of them say something derisive about people who actively tried to separate their appearance from mainstream culture, whether it was with tattoos, hair, piercings, or clothing. Being around BMX riders who always knew about the coolest styles and music reminded me of the value of outwardly rejecting the status quo. That hipness could become contrived, to be sure, but it was also a nod to fellow weirdos, a way to tell each other we weren't alone in the world.

Following Jason's lead, I started wearing Wranglers and skinny Levi's exclusively. They looked more punk than girl jeans, which, when flared, had this corny seventies vibe. In high school, we would've come to the conclusion that guys looked stupid in girl jeans together—but Jason got there without me. He also shaved his head. It had grown out a tiny bit, so it was this unwashed, fingernail-length black hair that looked endlessly cool. I shaved my head, too, which Natalie said looked hot.

We were all drinking in Natalie's apartment one night with a few of her friends from Boston when Jason got up and said he had to piss. He came back from the bathroom ten minutes later. We made eye contact, but then he sniffed and looked away, quickly wiping his nose. He sat farther away from Natalie's friend, Sarah, who was clearly into him. Jason wouldn't stop bouncing his leg, and his eyes darted around the room. I'd been around enough wastoids in Suffield to know he'd just sniffed cocaine. We went down to the building's courtyard to smoke, and I was able to take him aside.

"What, you're in Mötley Crüe now? Only douchebags do coke."

"Don't worry about it, Mrs. Thompson." He finished his cigarette and told me he was leaving. I didn't try to stop him, but I was on edge the next morning and couldn't concentrate on anything, waiting for him to text me back. Natalie knew I was worried about Jason, so she said, "Let's grab a coffee. My treat." She was putting in a lot of effort to not show jealousy over my friendship with him and to respect the fact that we'd been through so much together. I hadn't told her about Jason professing his love for me, and I didn't plan to.

I held her hand and tried to listen to her talk about bell hooks as we walked. Philly had a particular glow on warm summer days, and it was one of those days, when there was green sprouting up everywhere and life felt hopeful. Normally, I would've been happier than a hound dog in a henhouse (to borrow a saying from Jason's dad). But all I could think about was how badly I wanted my phone to vibrate.

"I'm sure he's fine," Natalie said, irritated. "Probably just hung over." She took a sip from her Americano and glanced at the hipster couple sitting at the table next to us.

"Yeah, I know. I just wish he wouldn't pull this shit." It was hard to resist the urge to pull out my phone and check it again.

Jason texted me two hours later to let me know he was alive. All he said was, "I'm okay, darling. Don't get your panties in a knot."

∿

In July, Jason went on a trip out west with the FBM team to film for their new video. I'd visited California on a family vacation years ago, but I would've much rather gone there on a riding trip. Dad hated crowds and lines, so I'm sure you can imagine how pleasant he was at Disneyland and Six Flags.

The FBM squad hit several legendary spots on the way to Cali, making a snaking route that would only make sense to BMX riders.

Jason called me after they rode with Chase Hawk[4] in Austin and same when they spent a few days in Salt Lake riding with Matt Beringer and Mike (fucking) Aitken. Beringer had converted his backyard into a BMX amusement park with trails, a rideable waterslide that shot you into the jumps, and a six-foot mini ramp. He also had a wacky bowl setup in his two-car garage that, Jason said, was super tight but fun once you figured out how to pump it. When Jason told me he tried acid at Beringer's and watched the tree out front turn into a waterfall of lizards, my stomach dropped. Jason's life was reaching in a different direction than mine, and that feeling of losing someone you love gutted me.

∿

When I'd applied to school and Mom recommended doing an English major, I thought, *Fuck yeah. All I'll have to do is read and write.* I'd long found refuge in books. I hated most of what we were supposed to read in high school, which is why I didn't do most of my reading assignments. I loved the stark grace of the writing in *The Old Man and the Sea*, and I connected with Holden Caulfield's caustic voice in *The Catcher in the Rye*—but that was pretty much it as far as liking any literature from my high school classes. Most of it was too old and stuffy for me to care. Instead of zoning out or getting antsy when I talked about what I was reading like Jason did, Natalie would ask me to expand on my thoughts and say more.

When I was in high school, my mom showed me books like *This Boy's Life*, *Less Than Zero*, and *On the Road*. From there, I found Burroughs, then Bukowski, then Hunter S. Thompson. Mom made sure to point out those writers' misogyny (in real life and their work), but I also loved how raw and unapologetic their writing was. They each had such distinct styles and voices but no

---

4   He's the only rider I've seen besides Jason who had so much bike control before he turned eighteen.

bells or whistles. It reminded me of my favorite riders, how people like Jason, Mike Aitken, and Chase Hawk could say so much with simple, fundamental tricks.

Mom thought I'd be an awesome teacher, to which I responded, "There's no way I can deal with those little assholes all day." Even still, she talked me into adding a secondary education minor.

The minor required me to complete service hours alongside a teacher in the classroom. I could apply for different schools, one of which was the Philadelphia Juvenile Justice Center. Most of my classmates thought it sounded like a nightmare, but it caught my interest. I applied and started helping out Natasha Swenson, a Black woman who taught in both the girls' and boys' units.

Although I initially balked at the idea of teaching, something clicked at the JJC. Some kids would try to string me along and get me to do their homework, and many would straight up refuse to do any work at all. After a while, some of the youth started to trust me enough to let me know where their reading and writing levels truly were, which was enough to make you want to throttle anyone who opposed fixing our broken, inequitable education system.

On my first day, this white kid looked me dead in the eyes and told me he'd rather punch me in the face than read a book. It seemed like he meant it. I was shaken, so Mrs. Swenson gave me some advice. "You really only have to worry about the youth hurting each other. And remember, you're on their side. Fuck the guards, at least most of them." She paused for a second. "Also, just to be straight up with you, don't fall for the white savior shit. You have to let go of your ego."

As we were cleaning up the classroom and Mrs. Swenson stepped outside the unit to smoke a cigarette, I saw a burly guard manhandle this scrawny Puerto Rican kid to the ground for refusing to mop and being a smartass about it. The kid mouthed, "Fuck you," when he finally grabbed the mop. Without saying anything, the guard wrestled him to the ground, holding him there face-first, his knee in the kid's back.

"How many times do I need to tell you, Morales? If you don't want to mop, you can stay in solitary for the next week."

"Yes, sir," the kid choked out. "Sorry, sir."

He was only thirteen. I was disgusted with myself for just standing there, watching it happen, but I didn't know what else to do.

I passed the guard's station on my way out. The guy looked at me and said, "That's the only way they'll learn, sometimes," and it was obvious what he meant: *Let's keep this between me and you.* I reported his stupid ass the next day. From then on, both the guards and the kids knew where I stood.

30

After a session at Posh in August, I went to my last party at Chunk House. Devin invited Mitch over, and Mitch was so stoked about it. He spiked his hair for the occasion and wore a hemp necklace with some sort of stoner orb on it. One of the first things Devin did was put Mitch in a headlock and mess up his hair, sending a flurry of gel flakes into the air. Mitch was short and muscly, built like a wrestler, but he was engulfed by Devin's bulk. Mitch knew he was the butt of every joke, but he was hanging out with a bunch of amazing riders he looked up to.

Throughout the night, Devin kept egging him on to drink more. "Hey, Misty," he said, "come do another beer bong with me."

"I'm good, man," Mitch responded, his eyes half open after taking substantial hits from a joint people were passing around. He slouched farther into the cigarette-burned orange couch next to the kitchen island, which was littered with wounded soldiers.

"Don't be a little bitch, Misty." Devin filled the beer bong. Cheap beer foamed in the red funnel and flooded the hose. "But I guess you would look hot in a dress."

I'd only had a few beers. I was watching this like a car wreck you know is about to happen but can't do anything to prevent. Or maybe I could've stopped it, and I was just a coward. Jason was laughing like a jackal.

Mitch tottered past the row of immaculate bikes that were flipped upside-down, resting on their seats, and into the bathroom. He dragged his hand across the Black Flag, G.G. Allin, and Anal Cunt posters hanging on the army green wall. Devin told us he was going to make Misty suck his dick, which everyone thought was hilarious. One of the guys got out his camera. Mitch came back out, looking like a dazed rabbit in oncoming traffic when he saw he was being filmed.

"Hey, Misty," Devin said, "remember how I told you we all suck each other off?" The entire house was in hysterics. Mitch looked at him with unfocused eyes. "If you suck my dick, I'll suck yours." Devin could barely speak he was laughing so hard.

"I don't know, man...I don't really swing that way." Mitch's words stretched out from his mouth like molten rubber.

"I thought I told you," Devin said. "It's not gay if it's only with your friends. It's just helping out your bros." The room erupted in laughter.

After a few more minutes of this, Mitch reluctantly got on his knees. Devin unbuckled his belt, its ironic rodeo buckle dangling in front of Mitch's face. Then, suddenly, Devin punched the top of his head with this horrible downstroke, knocking Mitch to the ground. The punch landed with a meaty thud, like a pack of ground beef getting dropped on the sidewalk. "You faggot," Devin said. "You were about to suck my dick."

The laughter in the room drowned out the blaring music. Mitch covered his head in his hands and stayed on the ground for a minute or two. Then he got up and, I shit you not, grinned and tried to laugh with everyone. He passed out on the orange couch within the next fifteen minutes, at which point Devin and Jason scrawled dicks all over his face with a black Sharpie.

I fell asleep watching *Gummo* in the living room with a few guys. I woke up early the next morning to the smell of stale beer and spilled bong water. Mitch was passed out with his mouth open, drooling on the couch, his face covered with a swarm of messily drawn cocks. I shook him awake. He looked at me from the bottom of an empty well. I helped him up, took him to the bathroom to help him wipe the marker off his face, and got him out to his car, a battered Nissan Altima covered in BMX stickers with a bike rack on the trunk. He looked at me before getting in, expecting me to say something. When I didn't, he said, "They go this hard on all new people?"

"No, dude. I'd honestly stay away if I was you."

He nodded like it was something he already knew but didn't want to admit, then got in his car and drove off. I left right after him.

On the drive back to Philly, I couldn't get Jason's cackling face out of my mind. I thought about the time in New York when he and I laughed along with Devin, Trevor, and Neb at the homeless man eating the pancaked candy bar; I thought about the countless times we'd watched videos like Uproot's *Laid to Waste* and giggled at riders mistreating people. I felt like a piece of shit for not distancing myself from that humor earlier on and for not stepping in and stopping what happened to Mitch. Part of me reasoned that Jason and I were simply mimicking the behavior of riders we idolized— but I didn't want to forgive myself so easily.

That afternoon, I told Natalie about Devin's antics. She said, "That asshole should be in prison."

31

I didn't call or text Jason back for two weeks after the party. That might not sound like much, but it was the longest we'd gone without speaking since we had become friends ten years earlier—over half our lives ago. Even though I needed space from him, I felt untethered.

He texted a few times, but I didn't answer. I finally decided to respond on a Saturday evening when he asked if I wanted to get up early the next day to meet two newly christened pros we knew, Troy and Gavin, in the Badlands, a pocket of neighborhoods in North Philadelphia. Most people were too scared to ride over there. Troy had found a playground with bank hips and ledges, as well as a perfect bank-to-rail only a block away. It was basically a skatepark.

When a guy at Catty told me where Troy and Gavin had been riding, he kept saying, "I can't believe they've been going to the ghetto to ride. They're nuts." It sounded like he was talking about someone exploring new frontiers of space, someone acting out of bravery rather than privilege. It was just some middle-class white kids going to an impoverished part of the city and feeling edgy because of it, but I didn't say this to him.

Jason drove down from Bethlehem and parked the Cutlass across the street from my apartment. I have no idea how he kept that car running, but it was still chugging along. We loaded our bikes into my truck and then stopped at McDonald's to grab breakfast. It was a gray Philly morning. The city was just waking up. Rubber and oil had been ground into the streets over the years, and those smells lingered in the air.

I tried to sip my coffee, but it was too hot. "You know Devin is a piece of shit, right?" I'd suddenly felt compelled to say it.

"Why? Because of that stuff with Mitch? He's just fucking around."

"That kid's going to be all fucked up. You can't just brush something like that off."

"Why do you care? That kid sucks. He's a moron."

"You can't treat people like that."

Jason shook his head, took the lid off his coffee, and blew into the scalding liquid. "You're all self-righteous now?" He found an Eyehategod CD in my case, put it in, and turned up the volume. We didn't say anything else on our way to the Badlands.

We found the elementary school where we were supposed to meet Gavin and Troy. Across the street was a small block of shops with an old laundromat, an insurance place, and a decrepit bodega. I parked. An older woman smoking a cigarette on her stoop looked at us like, *Why are you here?*

We got our bikes out of my truck and pedaled over to the playground after Troy and Gavin pulled up and parked behind us. Gavin and Jason aired the bank hips higher than what seemed possible. Troy did these long icepick grinds on the ledges, locking in and sliding in a way that made it look like he had Jedi control over his bike. Gavin went back to his car to get his camera, and they shot a few clips. We were about to head over to the bank-to-rail when we heard, "Give me that camera, motherfucker."

The guy looked like he was in his forties. He pointed an old twenty-two with a long barrel at Gavin. He wore an Eagles beanie pulled down low, and his Nike cross trainers were scuffed and worn.

The last thing in the world this guy wanted was to shoot anyone. Who knows if the gun was even loaded.

Jason looked at Gavin and said, "Don't give him anything." I couldn't believe he'd be so stupid about something replaceable like a video camera, even if it was expensive.

"Shut the fuck up, J," I said, then to Gavin: "Give it to him. Fuck the camera."

Jason shook his head in exasperation but didn't say anything else. A thousand-dollar camcorder was different to him than to me. I also thought he wanted to act tough in front of some fellow pro riders. Gavin handed over the camera. The guy told us to lie down and throw our wallets out. He picked them up and bolted.

It shook us up in the way things like this scare white kids from small towns and suburbs. I also couldn't help myself from wondering if we deserved to get robbed. We were on an adventure to ride our kids' bikes on new obstacles. People in the Badlands were just trying to live.

Transworld BMX ended up publishing a full article about our excursion a month after the fact. They called it "BMX in the Ghetto." I had just started my sophomore year of college. The writer interviewed Troy and Gavin, who talked about the mugging with the exaggeration you'd expect. They painted the guy like he was some crazed murderer we barely escaped.

"Don't you think that's bullshit?" I asked Jason after the article came out. We were hanging out at my and Harold's apartment, sharing a pizza after a session at FDR. "It wasn't like that at all."

"Who cares? They just told it like that for a good story."

"It's racist, though. The whole thing is basically about how we should be afraid of Black people."

"I don't know, dude. I think you're reading too far into it." Jason ate the last bite of his crust and grabbed another slice.

"We've been force-fed so much racial bias that we don't even realize it half the time," I said. "Trust me. That article is racist as fuck."

"I guess you'd be the one to know. I'm too stupid for all the lofty shit you and Natalie talk about, right?"

"What? I don't think that at all."

Jason stopped eating and sat quiet for a few moments, staring at the ground. "Fuck, sorry, Ry. I've just been feeling fucked up lately."

I apologized, too, although I wasn't quite sure why. "What's going on?"

He sighed. "Nothing, man. Just living away from home, I guess." There was more he wanted to say, but I didn't want to corner him, so I left it alone.

∿

"Piece of shit!" Jason picked up his bike and hurled it as hard as he could into one of the ledges. The abrasive sound of metal hitting concrete made my ears ring. His pedals left scratch marks on the ground.

A month after the Badlands article was published, we were riding Love Park, a famous skate spot just a short ride from my apartment. With its smorgasbord of ledges and stair sets, the place looked like a street plaza you'd find at a skatepark. Jason had been trying this icepick-manual-one-eighty line for over an hour.

He waited until a group of Russian tourists walked by and then tried again. And again. And again. One of the tourists turned around and snapped some photos of Jason acting like a jackass. The guy ate it up, tapping his friends on their shoulders and pointing at Jason.

"What the fuck have I done to deserve this?" Jason was screaming into the sky at the top of his lungs. I'd seen him chuck his bike a few times over the years, but nothing too aggro. This was another level.

Countless videos showed battle clips like this. And I got it. You knew exactly how the trick or sequence worked, but your body wouldn't cooperate. Sometimes, you could muscle it out after a long string of attempts. Other times, your legs and arms started to betray you, and it was maddening. I also knew there was more going on with Jason but that he'd say everything was good if I asked.

I still laughed at him. "What, you're Vic Ayala now?" Vic was known for his ridiculous, drawn-out meltdowns, his chest-puffing displays of anger.

Jason glared at me but couldn't maintain it. "Goddamn street, dude," he said with a forced chuckle. "This tech shit can drive you insane."

A group of five or six skaters rolled up and started skating the ledges. We knew the drill. It was an unspoken rule at Love that skaters got first dibs if they wanted it. Most of them weren't happy about riders scraping wax off the ledges with our pegs, despite the fact that it was completely ingrained into the concrete by now. One of the guys said something to his buddies we couldn't hear. They laughed, looking right at us.

"We should fuck those guys up," Jason said. It sounded bizarre coming from him. He'd never been in a fight.

"Are you kidding? That's always how it is at Love."

"I'm sick of getting pushed around by skaters." Jason kept his eyes locked on them.

"Dude, seriously, let's go. You're gonna get both of our asses kicked." I started pedaling away, but Jason rode over there. Worried about what he was going to do, I turned around and followed.

As Jason approached, one of the skaters loudly said to his buddy, "These douchebag bikers need to leave our ledges the fuck alone." He wore baggy cargo pants that sagged down past his ass, revealing plaid boxers. He was shorter than Jason but more sturdily built. He tried to ollie onto a ledge. He couldn't get up high enough, so only his front truck touched the concrete before he hopped off.

Jason threw down his bike, walked straight up to the guy, and shoved him. I'd never seen him do anything like that. "You can't even grind these ledges, you little bitch," Jason said. "Skaters are such fucking hypocrites. You whine about getting kicked out of street spots, but then you do the same exact shit to us." He balled his fists. Rage emanated from him like an electric field.

Without hesitating, the guy wound up and punched Jason squarely in the jaw. He staggered backward, hand on his chin, as the guy and his friends laughed and mocked him. "Fuck you, assholes," Jason said. Pushing back tears, he picked up his bike and pedaled away. I caught up to him on the sidewalk outside the park.

"What the fuck was that?" I said.

"Thanks for backing me up. You just stood there."

"Getting in a fight would never change those assholes' minds. It's pointless."

Jason's anger filled the air around us as we pedaled back to my apartment, a fury that, I knew, didn't have much to do with the skaters. They were just an excuse for him to let it out. We rode to his car, and he put his bike on the rack. He was about to get in without saying anything.

"You know you can talk to me, right?" I said. "You're freaking me out."

He sighed and opened the door. "It's nothing. Forget it." He started his car, put a Metallica CD in the stereo, cranked it, and drove off.

32

At the beginning of October, during our sophomore year, I brought Natalie up to meet Mom in New Haven and then Dad in Suffield. Mom fell in love with Natalie when she started telling her about school and her job, about what she was reading and what she planned to read next. Natalie just had this vibe that made you want to be around her all the time.

Since leaving Dad, Mom had embraced her inner bohemian. She began collecting classical records, playing them on an old turntable she bought at Goodwill. Posters with Einstein and Steven Hawking quotes decorated the walls of her one-bedroom apartment, which was on the second floor of a renovated Victorian rooming house. Ungraded papers with titles like "My Analysis of The Awakening" littered the side tables.

"Don't fuck it up with this one," Mom whispered to me as we cleared the table after dinner and Natalie watched TV. It was only the second or third time in my life I heard my mom drop an f-bomb. She'd been in the habit of not cussing in her classroom for so long that it usually stuck with her at home.

"I wasn't planning on it," I whispered back.

We started doing the dishes, me washing and Mom drying. She said, "How's J doing in Bethlehem?"

"Pretty good, I guess." I rinsed off a plate and handed it to her. "Partying too much, but he still rides all the time. Random kids recognize him at skateparks now."

"Tell him I said to stop drinking. Addiction runs in his family, his mom's side at least."

I told her I would, not sure if I'd follow through.

In Suffield the next day, I introduced Natalie to my dad, then brought her out to see our jumps in the woods. I'd talked about them countless times with her, showing her my and Jason's split part from the Manmade video as well as all the photos I had. We walked back there holding hands.

Showing her Orion, I said, "They look all fucked up now, but Jason and I had them running so smooth when we lived here. It was beautiful." Out of habit, I stomped my right foot on a lip to pack it.

"How long did all this take you?" She brushed a wisp of hair from her forehead.

I hadn't really thought about it that way, rather as this never-ending project. "Um…seven years, I guess?"

It was disconcerting to see our jumps in disrepair during the fall, a time when, not too long ago, they would've been in perfect condition. For years, our trails had been a sanctuary for Jason and me. The lips were supposed to be sharp and crisp, but they'd sunken in from the snow and rain the previous winter and spring. It scared me to think that an entire summer had gone by without us riding our jumps. There were chunks missing where the packed dirt had broken down and washed away.

I showed Natalie Battery and Harvester, pointing out the parts where you could transfer between the lines. I was staring at Orion, lost in thought, when she grabbed my hand and said, "Have you ever fucked anyone out here?" I swear I could about chew on my heart, it would leap so high into my throat when she said things like this.

∿

Some time apart had helped us, but Dad was still hesitant around me. He kept looking away when we made eye contact. He thought Natalie was great, but I have to admit I was bummed by how relieved he was that I'd brought a girl home. It was obvious to anyone who saw us together how much I loved her, and this delighted Dad to no end. Don't get me wrong. I was happy he liked her. I also kept picturing the exact opposite reaction I'd seen on his face when he caught me and Jason together almost two years earlier. I still hadn't told Natalie that story.

I showed her the house, my old room, and the ramp in the shop, which, to my surprise, Dad hadn't scrapped like I thought he would. His and Mom's wedding pictures still hung in the hallway leading to the bedrooms. Natalie looked at one of them laughing and cutting their gigantic cake. "Your mom looks gorgeous," she said. Mom's light brown hair was done up like Farrah Fawcett's, and her smile radiated light.

Dad grilled some steaks from a buck he'd recently killed. Natalie's brow crinkled as she chewed her first bite of venison. It took her a minute to process the unique tang of wild meat, as it's not really a flavor you encounter elsewhere. Watching her face, I laughed under my breath. She looked at me in a way that very clearly told me to shut the fuck up. While Dad asked Natalie about her family, I kept looking over to the empty chair where Mom would've been sitting.

As I was putting our bags in my truck the following morning, Dad took me aside and said, "I've been waiting for the right time to tell you this." He put his hands in his pockets and glanced down at his feet. "I've been saving to give you money for a house, or at least enough for a down payment, so you can pay the rest off without much of a problem." He looked at me expectantly, both of us desperately wishing this could fix everything.

"That's insane, Dad. I can't take that kind of money from you."

"It's already yours."

On the drive back to Philly, I told Natalie about my dad catching me and Jason in the tool room. I told her about punching my dad in the face and getting punched back. "That's the real reason my parents got a divorce," I said, my breath getting short. "Or at least that's the straw that broke the camel's back."

"Wait," she said skeptically, "I thought you said it was because of your dad's drinking."

I started to panic at her reaction and immediately felt guilty for not telling her the truth earlier. "It was so fucked. I wish it didn't happen—and I didn't want you to think my dad's some horrible bigot."

"I mean, I'm sorry that happened...I just wish you would've told me." Natalie got quiet, staring out the window at the quilt of fallen leaves that bordered the road. She asked me to pull over at the next gas station. She bought a pack of Camel Lights and smoked one before getting back in. She had quit smoking before I met her, so I'd never seen her take a drag. She inhaled deeply, exhaling smoke through her nose.

She didn't say much for the rest of the drive, but she forgave me after a few days. She said she did, at least. She never said it, but I got the feeling that me not telling her about the shop incident was my last big fuck up she could forgive.

∿

Two weeks later, Natalie invited me to stay at her parents' house. They lived in a gorgeous three-story brownstone in South Boston, near Cambridge. The red-brown bricks seemed to shine. The streets and sidewalks on their block looked as if they'd been scrubbed by hand, and there were Mercedes, BMWs, and Land Rovers parked along the curbs. I knew it would embarrass her, but I still said, "Jesus, Natalie. Your house is beautiful."

She scoffed and said, "Yeah, it's amazing how much money my dad has made by fucking people over." I could see her breath in the crisp air.

We got our bags from my truck, went inside, and put them in her room, which was pretty much exactly how I'd pictured it. She had a Le Tigre and Bikini Kill LP, both autographed by Kathleen Hanna, set side by side in a frame above her desk. Flyers from old hardcore shows were plastered up alongside abstract paintings she'd made in high school, which, as I suspected, were better than she let on.

"You saw Coalesce?" I said when I noticed the faded handbill. "You didn't tell me about that one."

"It was amazing. The guitarist looks like he's having a spiritual revelation when he plays."

Her parents wouldn't be home for a couple of hours, so I asked if I could go down on her. Her boldness had been rubbing off on me.

Throughout the weekend, I walked carefully through the halls, constantly worried I'd break some irreplaceable piece of art. Marble, wood, and steel sculptures, as well as expensive paintings, decorated every floor. Somehow, none of it seemed ostentatious or pretentious. I guess that's why Terry was a respected curator at ICA.

Natalie would shove me in the halls, or fake like she was going to. "If you break something, I'm telling your parents it was you,"

I said after barely dodging a side table with a small-but-expensive-looking copper sphere on it. This, of course, only made it funnier to Natalie.

We ate strawberry ice cream in front of the fireplace after dinner that night. Periodically glancing at the mess of colors in a chaotic abstract painting that hung on the wall behind the leather sofa, I told Mark and Terry about Jason smashing his face at FDR and some of our other injuries over the years.

"You guys at least wear helmets, right?" Terry asked. "Promise me you'll start wearing one. The brain is so fragile."

Like a broken record player, I told her we would, knowing it would never happen.

33

There was a big Halloween jam at the Little Devil warehouse. They booked a few bands, so I invited Natalie. She still hadn't seen us ride in person.

I felt self-conscious at first, like I was trying to show off. But then I got that glorious tunnel vision of the session when Jason did a beastly stall on the railing behind the sub-box, somehow springing back into the quarter pipe. I initially felt awkward seeing him because we hadn't talked since his blowout at Love Park—but that faded as we started riding. I blasted tables off the wall-ride, and I did one of the floatiest threes I've ever done over a box jump, nosing it like I was trying to piledrive my front end. Natalie's cheer cut above everyone else's. Nate Wessel lit a Roman candle and put it in his back peg; it shot off in the air when he jumped the box. When I looked over at Natalie to see her reaction, she rolled her eyes.

Following the session, the first band set up on the ground in front of one of the quarter pipes. While they played a set of dirty punk that reminded me of a grimier Hot Water Music, I went to take a piss. I refilled my beer from one of the kegs, and, when I came back, there were four dudes crowded around Natalie, trying to talk to her. It was another typical BMX party where guys outnumbered women at least five to one. I'd seen a few of the dudes around. I walked between two of them and put my arm around Natalie's shoulder. They melted back into the party when they realized I was her boyfriend.

"I would not want to be here on my own," Natalie said between songs. "But it was sick to finally watch you and Jason ride. I knew it was beautiful—I just didn't realize you guys went so high."

We woke up in her apartment. She told me about going to parties in Boston with guys from the hardcore scene, parties where she was one of only a few women, parties where older straight-edge guys would hang out and hit on drunk girls who were still in high school. Tendrils of sunlight reached through the blinds and danced in her brown eyes. Tucking her hair behind her ears, she said, "I never stopped loving the music, but I got so tired of feeling like prey." She told me about one of the last hardcore shows she went to—Ramallah in Boston—and how, after she went to the bathroom and came out, this dude kept asking for her number. He followed her around and stared at her for the entire show. "I saw Le Tigre in New York not long after that, and it was a completely different world. I felt totally safe."

"That's so fucked. I'm sorry it was like that."

"It's a bummer. That music got me through a lot, like when those girls at school were bullying me and saying all that racist shit on IM. I could let out all my rage at hardcore shows, but then I felt like dudes like that took it away."

That semester, I was in a feminist lit course with a teacher who never hesitated to point out male-brain bullshit. I went to her office one afternoon to talk about an upcoming paper. She saw my Standard shirt and asked if I rode.

"You know about BMX?" I asked.

She said her brother used to ride. "I always thought they looked so cool, and I wanted to do it so badly. But I didn't think girls belonged in that world. It would be interesting for you to think about how that could change."

I didn't need any convincing to write my term paper on BMX. What I didn't expect was to watch my perception of the culture that shaped me get further upended as I wrote—and then to realize how obvious those flaws had always been for anyone who wasn't a dude. I thought about the FBM rider writing on that girl's ass in New York and Trevor repeatedly telling her to fuck Jason. I thought about how I could count on one hand the times I saw women riders in BMX videos and magazines. I thought about the punk girls who sometimes hung out at Chunk House and how often they looked over their shoulders, especially when they went to the bathroom. Walking across campus to hand in my paper, I remember thinking, *I'll always love riding my bike, but the culture is fucked.*

34

Although things were strained between me and Jason, I couldn't stop thinking about him in that way, about his sinewy body and how we made each other feel. To me, he was an artist whose incredible skill only made him that much more attractive. I also longed for those moments of dumb humor between us when I could relax and get a break from trying to be smart. At the same time, I felt sure that Natalie was who I should end up with. She challenged me to push my thinking, which I'd been craving for a long time—*and* she was a sexual dynamo, constantly making me feel like I was on the verge of exploding, sometimes just by holding my hand. She and Jason fulfilled totally different parts of me. I started wondering if there was a way to have them both.

During the spring semester, I discovered a reality TV show called *Poly* that followed a handful of people in polyamorous relationships. Its representation of polyamory definitely didn't come from a genuine place, as the show could often feel like cheap, softcore porn. But there was also a triad of two guys and one woman. They were a bit out there—New Age San Diego people who believed in the healing properties of crystals—but they seemed happy. Why couldn't that be us?

Natalie loved reality TV, too, so I brought over one of the *Poly* DVDs I'd rented. She got fully into it, following the triad's ups and downs and watching them try to navigate a world where they constantly had to explain and justify their lifestyle.

"What if me, you, and Jason were in a relationship together?" I said almost accidentally, the words slipping from my mouth. We were lying in her bed, watching on her computer.

"What if I lock you in a room and make you listen to Creed for a week?" She grabbed the edge of her blanket and playfully rubbed it on my face.

"No, really, though, what would it be like, do you think?"

"Wait. You're serious?" She sat up, pulled her knees close to her chest.

"I mean…I'm not *not* serious."

"I thought we've been through this. If you want to fuck around with Jason, that's fine. But I wouldn't be okay with it if we're still together."

"But we'd all be together…and we could do stuff together." I tried to hold her hand, but she recoiled.

"That sounds horrible. If I'm not enough for you, maybe we should take a break."

The thought of losing Natalie was a blade in my intestines. But I was transfixed by the idea that I could have everything I wanted. "I think you'd like it if you gave it a chance," I said.

She kept her knees pressed against her chest and didn't look at me. Her voice wavering, she said, "I think you should leave."

"I'll drop it. I'm sorry."

"I just want to be alone tonight."

When I tried to hug her, she turned away. I left, stepping over puddles of melted snow as I walked to my truck, which was parked a block from her apartment. There was no one around, so my footsteps seemed louder than they actually were. On the phone the next day, Natalie said, "You need to figure out what you want. I'm done with the back-and-forth bullshit."

"No, I want to be with you. You're it for me." But there was uncertainty beneath my words, and we both knew it.

She was quiet for a moment, and in that silence, I knew her answer—and also that there was no convincing her otherwise. When Natalie made up her mind about something, that was usually the end of the story. "I think we need a break," she said.

After she hung up, I wept, feeling like no matter what I did, I was going to lose someone I loved.

35

Natalie and I exchanged a few messages on Myspace over the next few weeks, but neither of us said much. Hard as it was, I resisted my impulse to bombard her with calls and texts, as I knew that would only push her further away. I wanted her back, but I began questioning if the right relationship had been staring at me all along: should Jason and I be together?

Outside of my fantasies, things were still awkward between him and me. We were both trying to decide what to do about our attraction to each other, as it obviously hadn't faded. When we rode together, the weirdness dissipated. As bummed as I'd been about BMX culture, I never got tired of the ecstasy of riding dirt jumps and, to a lesser extent, skateparks and street. My anxiety always came back, but it wasn't as overwhelming in the wake of a good session.

Not long after Natalie told me she wanted a break, I met up with Jason at Posh. He told me that Rob Johansson, a legendary filmer and editor, asked him to film a full part for a new trail-heavy video called *Old Glory*. Johansson wanted street and park in there as well—but, in the spirit of the videos he made in the early nineties that gave him his start, he wanted dirt to be the primary focus. With a lineup of Mike Aitken, Justin Inman, Chris Doyle, Chase Hawk, and a few more of the world's finest riders, getting asked to do a part for *Old Glory* was like someone from *The New Yorker* soliciting your writing.

"I want to film most of my part on a road trip across the country," Jason told me between runs. "Just me and you, this summer. Can you do it?" We were sitting on our bikes, lined up to hit the Speedball line. There was desperation in his voice, like the possibility of me saying no terrified him.

We had never been on a long riding trip together. It seemed like an opportunity to mend our relationship—and to get out of my head for an extended period of time. I was constantly reminded of Natalie, whether through songs that came up when I put my iPod on shuffle, or when I passed restaurants and coffee shops we'd been to together, or when I read a book I knew she'd like.

"Fuck it," I told Jason. "Let's do it."

Watching *Wild at Heart*, Natalie's favorite movie, later that evening, I wondered if I should call her and tell her about the trip. But I decided against it. I was still trying to give her space, and I knew telling her would only make her worry.

I didn't have student assistant hours at the JJC until September. As far as responsibilities, all I had to worry about was my bullshit job at the pizza place. I told my boss I needed three weeks off in June. He shot me down. It was an easy decision to quit. The thought of not having to deal with the bros who frequented that place, not to mention the one who owned it, made it hard not to smile like an asshole when I put in my two weeks' notice.

Jason and I planned to do our trip like a mix between a punk tour and an extended camping trip: crash at people's houses when we could and sleep in a tent when we couldn't. Worst case scenario was that we'd have to put our bikes in the cab of my truck and sleep in the flatbed, which wouldn't be too bad because of the camper shell.

Excited as a little kid waiting for Christmas, I couldn't sleep for two weeks leading up to our excursion. When we got back home, I sat down and wrote out what happened each day, as if putting it on the page could somehow change it.

—

6/19

We packed up my truck and drove down to this bowl in DC, where Jason proceeded to blast what must've been eight-foot airs. Some skaters showed up and whined about bikes not being allowed, even though we weren't using our pegs on their precious coping. We said fuck them and, wanting to clock some distance, drove the nine hours to Louisville. I'd never driven through West Virginia. It was endless mountains of green. We saw many mullets of differing varieties and far more Confederate flags than the world has ever needed (which is none). I thought about Natalie, but it wasn't accompanied by the savage tug on my guts that I'd been feeling at home—maybe because I was also anticipating being alone with Jason for the next few weeks.

Pulling into Louisville, I thought about how rad it would be to see a Breather Resist show, but that was wishful thinking. Natalie said they're one of the best live bands she's seen. Jimmy Levan put us up for the night. I'd never met him, but Jason knew him. His voice sounded like he gargled gravel in the morning, and he had his blonde hair cut into this ridiculous fashion mullet. He and Jason got shitfaced on some garbage whiskey, but I knew they'd both ride beautifully in the morning.

6/20

We woke up and headed straight to the new Louisville skatepark. Jimmy ripped that place a new asshole, riding the full pipe like it wasn't a twenty-four-foot monolith. Within the first ten minutes, Jason was flowing like he'd been riding there for years.

Jimmy gave us Dan's number, who had some jumps near his house in Nashville. After riding in Louisville for a few hours, we drove to Nashville and ate at a BBQ spot with Dan that made me want to sleep for a week. Dan took us to his jumps, which were nothing special, then Jason decided he wanted to see the Country Music Museum. The sections on Hank Williams and Johnny Cash were epic. Looking at the Hank Williams stuff, I couldn't stop thinking about Scott. I'm sure it was the same for Jason. I wanted to say something to him about how much I still miss his dad, but nothing sounded right in my head.

Wanting to cover some road, we drove three hours to Memphis, or at least right outside of it, where we found a random place in the woods to pitch our tent (no pun intended).

After we'd wrapped ourselves in our respective sleeping bags, Jason started laughing and said, "I told my mom I'm gay. She just said, 'No shit, Sherlock. I've known for years.'"

"She's the fucking best."

He inhaled sharply. "I didn't know if I should tell you, but I dated a guy in Bethlehem over the winter."

I felt a stab of jealousy. "That's rad, J. I'm happy for you."

"But it got all fucked up. I didn't want my roommates or any other riders to know, so I wouldn't go out in public with him." The inside of our tent was pitch black. Jason's voice seemed to rise from the ground. "He broke it off within a month."

I tried not to sound too excited. "That sucks. Sorry to hear it."

"Fuck it, I'll find someone else." He paused for a moment. "Do you think you'll marry Natalie?"

"We're taking a break. I don't know what's going to happen."

"Oh shit, why?"

By way of an answer, I unzipped his sleeping bag and kissed him.

I woke up to sunlight coming through the green canopy, illuminating Jason's face. Then guilt flooded my veins as I thought about Natalie. I lay on my back, staring at the tent's canvas and breathing deeply to calm myself. When Jason woke up, he started rolling up his sleeping bag and getting his stuff together like nothing had happened the night before. Not sure what else to do, I followed his lead. We bought coffee and Hostess doughnuts at a gas station, filled up my truck, then got back on the road.

We thought about going to Graceland but realized we both thought Elvis was bullshit, so we drove to Dallas. I'd never been to Texas. We drove through dusty plains, but there were also more forested areas than I expected. I couldn't stop replaying the previous night in my head.

It was hot and humid as fuck. We had to get some caffeine in our asses to get the energy to ride. We didn't know anyone in Dallas, so we just cruised around downtown, looking for spots. We found some rails at a municipal building. Jason icepick grinded a fifteen stair, locking in and actually sliding most of it. I double-pegged the twelve stair rail on the other side. We got kicked out by a security guard who called us dirty reprobates.

Since we were so close to Austin, we decided to drive down but, of course, left during rush hour like dumbasses, so it took us forever to actually get on the road. We were staying at the Ratty House, where Chase Hawk lived with some other riders. Jason and I knew going in that they're heavy into the bisexual scene. A party was in full swing when we pulled up.

We were on the back porch when I started to feel the warmth of the beer in my face. Jason went into one of the back rooms with two of the guys without even looking at me. I felt betrayed, but I didn't know if I had any right to feel that way. Another guy asked me if I wanted him to suck me off. Instead, I went into the bathroom alone and fantasized about having a threesome with Natalie and Jason—about the mechanics of it, who would do what.

Afterward, I tried to fall asleep on a couch with foam sticking out of its many rips, but I couldn't get past how Jason didn't try to get me involved. It didn't seem like he even considered it. Gnarly grindcore blasted from a stereo next to the kitchen, and people laughed maniacally in the backyard at I don't know what. Wanting to be alone, I went to my truck, which was parked on the street in front of the house, and fell asleep in the passenger seat.

6/22

I woke up to Jason knocking on the window. "What the fuck?" he said. "I've been looking all over the house for you."

"It was loud as fuck in there, so I came out here for some quiet."

"Whatever, weirdo. You ready to go? Everyone is going to go get coffee, then head to Ninth Street."

He seemed so nonchalant. I'm not sure how I wanted him to respond after the night in the tent—like something happened, I guess. I tried to brush it off and enjoy the fact that we were in one of the main BMX hubs in America. There were pros everywhere there. We ran into a few riders from the Kink team at the coffee shop. Around them and the Ratty House guys, Jason didn't step out of smartass mode and acted jaded about everything. It irritated the shit out of me.

Chase destroyed the Ninth Street jumps, blasting everything with tough fluidity. Watching him and Jason ride together was like watching Pippen and Jordan feed off each other. They were on a totally different planet than everyone else.

Jason ripping Ninth Street

Things got wild at Ratty House that night. I didn't feel like getting wasted, so it all had an edge to it. This crazy dude smashed a metal chair on the ground, and most of the riders disappeared into the bedrooms. Jason at least invited me to join this time, but it seemed like an afterthought, like he didn't care either way. Chase and another rider had recently started a sludge band. They jammed some dirty shit in the garage before the neighbors called the cops.

I knew I'd be driving in the morning. Jason was incoherent by the end of the night. He wouldn't shut up about how this guy who lived upstairs had the biggest dick he'd ever seen. "It's unreal," he said. "It looks like a baby's arm. You would've loved it. Why didn't you come?" His voice was childlike in his drunkenness.

"We have a long drive tomorrow," I said. "Shut up and go to sleep."

"Are you mad at me?"

"Just tired. We have to hit it early tomorrow morning."

Jason mumbled for a few more minutes before passing out. I was obviously jealous, but it also worried me to see him so drunk. He seemed out of control.

6/23

I woke up too early and got Jason's still-drunk ass up. We debated staying another day in Austin but decided to say fuck it and stick to the plan. We white-knuckled it to Albuquerque—an eleven-hour drive through barren desert. I drank an unholy amount of coffee and Mountain Dew and made it farther than I thought I'd be able to by the time Jason was finally sober enough to drive. I wanted to ask him exactly what he'd done with the guys at Ratty House, and I wanted to ask him about us. But I kept quiet.

"Don't try to tell me you're not pissed," Jason said as he drove out of a rest stop where we stopped to pee.

"Why would I be pissed?"

"That's what I'm trying to figure out."

In some paranoid corner of my mind, I wondered if he'd acted that way at Ratty House to get me back for being with Natalie. I tried to brush it off, telling myself he wouldn't do that, but the thought was a barnacle on my brain. "I've just been driving too much," I told him. "Fried from the road."

"Whatever you say," Jason said. "Put on some Sabbath or something." I put in Vol. 4, and he pumped the volume, not turning it down until we were close to Albuquerque.

We stayed with some dude named Travis, who Jason had met the previous summer. He came out of his apartment building to show us where to park. We grabbed our bags from the cab and shut the door to my truck.

"You're not leaving your bikes in there, are you?" Travis asked. He had greasy skin and a skeevy goatee.

"My camper shell is locked," I said.

"This place is tweaker central," he said. "Bring them in."

6/24

ABQ was the land of empty drainage ditches. We rode two before we even ate lunch, then we rode two more before nightfall. I was able to disconnect from the messiness between Jason and me during the sessions, honing my thoughts down to trying to go as high as possible on the wall-rides. Travis chain-smoked Marlboro Reds. I couldn't understand how he rode so well all day, like the cigarettes didn't slow him down at all. When he talked, his ashtray breath unfurled like a disgusting carpet.

Back at his place, Travis put in the new Props DVD. "You guys like to get low?" he asked, smiling like a dumbass.

"Fuck yeah," Jason said.

Travis went to his room and came back with a prescription bottle of OxyContin. He crushed a few pills with the butt of a butter knife, then he and Jason blasted some lines. I'd never watched anyone do real drugs before. Jason's green eyes looked black, just totally vacant. After Travis passed out, Jason absently rubbed me through my jeans, but then he stopped, put his head on my shoulder, and passed out. I felt sick to know he was messing with opioids.

6/25

I started in on Jason right off the bat that morning, and I didn't pull punches.

"Why are you fucking with that stuff? You know you have an addictive personality."

"Good God, Ry. It's such a small deal. Booze is honestly worse." He put in a Slayer CD and cranked it, but I didn't want to drop it. I turned the stereo back down.

"We used to talk so much shit about the wastoids in Suffield. Now you're becoming one of them."

"You think I don't know you're pissed from the Ratty House shit?"

He caught me off guard. "I don't care what you do," I stammered.

"Bullshit. It's like you just expect me to leap into your arms after you've been with someone else for the past year."

I hated how on point he was. I felt exposed, like I'd shown up to class naked. I almost told him to fuck off. Instead, I cut the bullshit. "I thought that's what you wanted."

"It was…" He stared at the road. "But I'm not sure anymore. I want things to be like they used to."

"Me too."

We didn't know what else to say to each other, so we just listened to Slayer's violent thrash until we got close to Phoenix and Jason asked me to read the directions Gonz, who we were meeting up with, had texted.

Jason told me Gonz was insane, but I guess nothing can really prepare you for a large man wearing white jeans and a cowboy hat riding street like it's his last night on earth. Gonz smoked crack with some random people downtown and tried to get me to do a backwards grind down this insane rail. He kept saying, "Ryan, my man, I know you're packing that big dick. You got this!"

He told us we could stay at his place, but we decided to drive to San Diego. Apparently, crack smoking was too gnarly even for Jason. About an hour outside Phoenix, he dozed off. My thoughts gravitated toward Natalie. I wondered if Jason and I could be a real couple, or if it would always be loose and open-ended. Natalie pushed me intellectually, and she constantly surprised me. But what if I'd fucked everything up with her? What if she had already found someone else? These questions were pistons in my brain, sending too much fuel to my nervous heart.

I woke Jason up when we got close to San Diego. He didn't know anyone there, so we decided to set up our tent on the beach. I was sure someone would kick us out, but we somehow didn't get hassled. Jason rolled over in his sleeping bag, leaving me to listen to the drone of waves. I felt like I needed to call Natalie. As I unzipped the tent, Jason asked me where I was going.

"Uh, I'm just going to call Natalie."

He was quiet for a second. "Oh…okay," he said, lying back on his pillow.

It was past 2:00 a.m. back in Philly, so my call went to voicemail. I hadn't heard Natalie's voice in weeks. "Hey, Natalie, it's me, Ryan," I said like an idiot. "I'm on a BMX trip with Jason and was thinking of you. Call me back if you want." I hung up before I could embarrass myself more.

I kept thinking about what Jason said, how I just expected him to pick up where we left off like nothing happened. I felt like an asshole because that's what I expected of Natalie, too. Maybe I didn't deserve either of them.

6/26

Jason drove so I could get some extra sleep. We went to the Sheep Hills jumps in Costa Mesa and met up with the infamous Sean Engstrom. Within two minutes of meeting him, he said, "I fucked a junky whore last night and got in a fight with my mom." Jason laughed like it was the funniest thing he'd ever heard.

It was awesome to ride Sheep after seeing it in so many videos and magazines over the years. It was a fun spot for sure, just super dusty. Sean drank Jim Beam all day and still rode like a beast. Jason and I both took a couple pulls with him because when else were we going to drink whiskey with Sean Engstrom at Sheep Hills? After I took a drink, Sean grabbed the bottle and said, "No, man, you gotta suck on it like a titty." He chugged a third of the bottle, then belched. I laughed in spite of myself. Maybe stupid shit like this was exactly what I needed.

We stayed with Sean at his apartment and got wasted on Captain Morgan. Then we got bored and walked around his neighborhood in Huntington Beach, tearing mailbox posts out of yards and pissing on cars. Sean took a shit in a fry container and threw it on the windshield of this lifted truck with a huge Metal Mulisha sticker on the back window. We're lucky we didn't get beaten up or arrested.

We'd been planning to ride street in LA, but Sean told us it was a bust and took us to Heath Pinter's house in Riverside instead. I felt like shit and had to pull over to puke, but I was good after I drank a bunch of Gatorade and ate some pretzels. I understood the desire to drown emotion in booze, as it obviously worked, but it was a Band-Aid on a broken bone. I was tempted to say something like that to Jason but thought better of it.

Along with Ninth Street, Heath's trails were the best we rode on the trip, although the dirt had sand in it that destroyed your skin if you wrecked. Heath had to water his jumps every day to keep them rideable. The main line had this cool step-up jump you could blast the fuck out of. Jason one-eightied it and somehow rolled out. I would never say this to him, but I felt like I was watching an artist every time he rode.

Riverside was only three hours from Vegas, so we drove to the outskirts and got a room at Motel 6. We were supposed to be Black Flag on this trip, but we both needed to sleep in a bed, not to mention shower in a bathroom that wasn't a biohazard. I'm not going to lie: I was excited about having Jason all to myself. At the same time, thoughts of Natalie wouldn't let up.

After we both took showers, though, we collapsed, each on our respective beds. I turned on the TV.

"I'd ask you to suck my cock," Jason said, smirking, "but I'm too tired to move." It was both a joke and an honest admission. As hungry as I was for his body, doing anything beyond lying in bed suddenly seemed impossible.

I started playing the TV game instead. We invented it years ago when we were bored. You hit mute, say something ridiculous, then press unmute and see how your dialogue fits in. I found a golfing tournament on ESPN.

"Another gorgeous swing from David Toms."

Mute.

"Now I'm hard as a rock and waiting for..." I said, giggling.

Unmute.

"*…a short putt into the hole.*"

We died laughing.

6/28

It was hot in Riverside and Albuquerque, but Vegas might as well have been the surface of the sun. It was too hot to ride by eleven. Aaron, who we stayed with, said people there only rode early in the morning and late at night. Luckily, we were able to get in a session at this awesome ditch with massive wall-rides and hips before the sun started cooking us like turkeys. It blew my mind to think that engineers designed these things that were so perfect for riding without having any idea that's what people would do with their creations.

Vegas gave me weird-ass vibes, and I couldn't see why anyone would want to live there. The strip was pretty much what you'd expect, and the rest was kind of like Phoenix: spaced out with a bunch of stucco and strip malls.

We went to Aaron's apartment to escape the heat and cool off. He asked us if we wanted to go to an eighteen-plus strip club after we downed a bunch of water. "The bitches there are out of hand," he said.

"You're not supposed to say the B-word around Ryan." Jason mockingly waved his hands like it was a big deal. "It's offensive," he said with a lisp. He and Aaron laughed.

"Eat a dick," I said. "I just think strip clubs are greasy." I hated that my trying to care about the world outside BMX was just a target of mockery for Jason. It's one of the things I used to love about him that now drove me up the wall: it was hard to get past his tendency to joke about everything. Who knew what it was like inside his head, though. He'd been through such heavy shit.

"Damn, okay," Aaron said. "You guys want to smoke a bowl and watch Dumb and Dumber instead?"

"Load 'er up," Jason responded.

When it finally cooled down enough to ride, we went to the YMCA skatepark. Jason wanted to clock footage, so he was roasting everything like there was no tomorrow. His body and bike fused during those moments, becoming a singular entity of serrated elegance. As I watched him ride, it was so clear that this was how he dealt with emotional strife. Sometimes I forgot when we weren't on our bikes. He let turmoil flood his body, putting it back in the world as beauty.

We closed out the night at this huge curved wall-ride. You could pedal as fast as you wanted at that thing, and, once you were locked in, you just carved it and let the wall shoot you off. Jason blasted inverts out of it, landing both tires on the concrete, perfectly. He also one-eightied out at a ridiculous height. It's hard to capture in words how incredibly he was riding. Even his smallest movements were laced with grace and aggression.

Jason tearing around the curved wall-ride in Vegas

We woke up early to shoot some more clips on the curved wall-ride, then we headed out to Salt Lake. About halfway there, I told Jason to put in Sabbath, not thinking much of it as he pulled Paranoid out of my CD case. When "Iron Man" came on, he said, "You ever think about my dad, Ry?"

"All the time."

Jason broke down as he said, "I used to think he was such a fucking coward. Sometimes, I still do. But now I mostly think about all the stuff we didn't get to do together." It was intense, but he seemed relieved to say it out loud. I didn't know what to say, so I just put my hand on his shoulder. It was the most he'd ever talked to me about Scott's suicide. We listened to the rest of Paranoid without saying anything. I knew we were both picturing Scott playing air guitar with a wrench.

Huge mountains surrounded the Salt Lake area. If I were an asshole, I'd call them majestic. We met Beringer and Aitken at the Layton skatepark, which they said was one of the best in Utah. I hadn't met either of those guys before. Considering his Slayer fandom and Trans Am, I half-expected Aitken to be this wild hessian, but he was actually pretty quiet and laid back. His riding was obviously hessian, though. In videos, you got a sense of how fast he snapped each movement. Watching him in person, it looked like he was doing some kind of martial arts on his bike.

We went to Beringer's house afterward and rode his backyard. There were a bunch of dudes there, partying and riding. Pictures and videos didn't do that place justice. It was a BMX playground, sitting somewhere between a joke and art. But the yard flowed together somehow. The waterslide got you going faster than you expected, shooting you into a curved wall that brought you around to a couple jumps. And that was just the beginning.

Beringer's yard

From my spot on top of the half-pipe, I noticed a pack of guys surrounding two women next to the firepit, so I stopped riding to stare at them—to let them know I was watching. It was a tactic I'd learned from Natalie.

Jason took a run, then positioned himself next to me and sat on his bike. "Don't ruin this with the white knight shit." He was speaking under his breath. "Take it easy." He put his hand on my shoulder like he was talking sense into me.

I glared at him and then looked back to the girls, who were getting ready to leave. Once they were gone, I was able to get back into the session. I was still frustrated with Jason, though.

Beringer had a guest room for riders who came through on road trips. Before we fell asleep, I thought about calling Jason out for being an asshole. I thought about trying to tell him that misogyny and homophobia are worm-eaten apples off the same poisoned tree of masculinity, but I knew he'd think I was being pretentious and condescending—and he'd be right. Not for the first time, I wished nothing existed for us outside riding. There was so much back and forth between us on the trip. I felt both closer to and more distant from Jason than I ever had.

6/30

We went to Salt Lake to get lunch with Aitken at a cool spot. Salt Lake freaked me out, though. The religion was so in-your-face. Temples were everywhere, the biggest one literally in the center of the city. I'd never seen so many blonde, blue-eyed people in my life. I once saw a documentary on MTV about this gay Mormon guy whose parents forced him to go to horrific "conversion" courses in a cruel attempt to turn him straight. It was aversion therapy with gay porn. Looking at the oppressive towers and gold statues in the middle of downtown, it was all I could think about.

We parked and met up with this dude, Elf, to ride street. He reminded me of Vic and Edwin when they rode NYC. He bump-jumped and grinded things most riders wouldn't even see. We ate pizza near the University of Utah, and Elf invited us to stay at his house. Getting stoned with Elf and his girlfriend, Jason took a bong hit, pulled me toward him, and shotgunned it into my mouth. As he breathed smoke into my lungs, his tongue danced on mine. It was as hot as it was confusing.

I felt awkward, so I took a few bong hits to smother it, even though I've never liked weed much. It must've been strong stuff because suddenly everything was funny as shit, and I was rolling around on the ground.

7/1

We woke up early to ride the Hell Hole, a full pipe in Wyoming. It was right on the Utah/Wyoming border, just outside this town called Evanston. You couldn't buy real porn, beer, or fireworks in Utah, so Evanston had a shitload of porn shops—and fireworks and liquor stores. They had warehouses of that shit.

Anyway, the Hell Hole was sick. Most of it was banked wall-rides you could carve super high on, but the end section was a huge spillway transition. Jason did fastplants at a stupid height, and he made the highest tire marks on the main wall-ride spots, climbing the cement like a lizard. There were a bunch of shitty tags inside the full-pipe, like marijuana leaves and anarchy symbols, so we knew the local kids liked to come out there to get wrecked. Before I could hesitate and let the impulse pass, I grabbed Jason and pulled him toward me. His moans echoed through the pipe. I didn't know what it meant, and I didn't feel like figuring it out.

We drove through Wyoming on I-80. It was bleak, but you could see these insane mountains in the background, so that part was cool. It was a relief when we finally got into Colorado and saw the trees. Jason tried to get every trucker we passed to blow his horn. As we approached one semi, he said, "Let's see if I can get a blowie from this guy, too." He giggled like an asshole. I tried to laugh even though I wanted to slap his face for joking about what happened in the full pipe.

We went to an indoor park in Colorado where we met some rad locals. We were planning to camp out, but two of the riders, Jared and Bryan, invited us to stay at their parents' house. Their mom fed us enchiladas and gave us fuzzy blankets to sleep in. I fell asleep on the couch within seconds of closing my eyes.

7/2

Denver was only an hour's drive from Fort Collins, which was a relief. Jason and I were both looking and feeling haggard, with our greasy hair and bloodshot eyes. Unless we were on our bikes, I felt sluggish as hell from all the driving, sleep deprivation, and fast food, not to mention the emotional tumult.

We had originally planned to ride the Denver skatepark, but the Fort Collins guys said it was too slick and took us to this skatepark in the suburbs that had an amazing bowl with perfect hips. We met this dude named Josh, who looked and rode like Sergio Layos, with his curly hair and buttery style. Josh smoked Black & Milds like cigarettes and listened exclusively to black metal. When he found out we had a tent, he got a few of his buddies together and took us camping in the woods.

We hung out around the campfire and jammed out to Pantera. It was so rad to genuinely bond with people through BMX. I'd been fixating on the negative aspects, but this was part of the culture, too, and it was worth holding onto.

7/3

Driving, Jason and I started playing this game we called Sausage, where you took turns trying to say absurd shit to make the other person laugh. The goal was not to laugh. I could get pretty stoic, but then Jason started doing this creepy baby talk that destroyed me every time. "Widdle baby gonna make a potty on my crusty peter?" was one of many highlights.

The plains in Kansas seemed to stretch on forever. Some of the one-stop towns had porn shops right off the highway. Without fail, we saw a billboard near each one that said something like, "Porn destroys families," or, "Real men don't do porn." It was funny but also depressing that people actually believed that bullshit. I'm sure the people who paid for those signs were huge fans of bisexuality.

We went to a crappy skatepark in Kansas City and decided to backtrack a half hour to Lawrence to ride the university. We found a handful of rails but nothing too cool before we got kicked out. We decided to say fuck it and drove the four hours to St. Louis, where Jason knew this guy, Paul, who had some cool trails. He didn't seem to mind that we rolled in past midnight. Paul had a husky named Emilio that wouldn't stop trying to hump me. Before I went to bed, I decided to call Natalie. It was late again, but she picked up. Jason eyed me when I slipped out the back door, then looked away when I turned my head toward him.

Natalie's voice was water in the desert. I told her about some of the places we rode, and she told me about how nice it had been to just lie around for the summer, reading whatever she wanted and picking up extra hours at the bookstore. My heart skipped when she said, "I miss you."

"I miss you so much," I said. "You have no idea."

"Well," she said, laughing nervously and talking in a mock bro voice, "call me or something when you're back in town."

7/4

We rode Paul's jumps in the morning. I was still buzzing from talking to Natalie. Jason sulked until we started riding. I guess Paul usually rode alone because no one in the area wanted to ride real jumps. There were two main lines that flowed through the trees, and you could transfer between them. Jason started doing these gorgeous nac nac X-ups, which I'd never seen anyone do, not like that.

Jason, nac-nac X-up at Paul's

We ate lunch and decided to head up to Chicago a day early. Paul had a few days off for the holiday, so he drove up with us in his own car. After a pit stop at a gas station, Jason took over driving so I could sleep. I put my sweatshirt against the window and rested my head on it. I was about to close my eyes when Jason asked, "Are you and Natalie getting back together?"

"I don't know." The words were heavy on my tongue.

He was quiet for a moment, then he said, "You guys make each other so goddamn happy." He wiped his eyes when he thought I wasn't looking. "It's honestly pretty gross," he said with a forced laugh.

I wanted to tell him I was still in love with him—to tell him that, in my heart of hearts, I wanted to build a life with him and Natalie, both. But I knew it could never be, so I didn't say anything else.

It was dark by the time we pulled up to KP's place in Chicago. We bought some fireworks in Wyoming, so we ran around his backyard, shooting Roman candles at each other.

7/5

KP took us to the Garden jumps, then we went to a party after riding all day. I downed some shots while Jason got fully wasted and started making out with another rider, right in the open. The muscular guy playfully pulled Jason toward a back room. To my surprise, Jason asked if I wanted to join. I followed before I could talk myself out of it.

For a few minutes, we were an intertwined mass, then Jason got on the bed and told the guy to fuck him. We'd never gone that far together, so I was taken aback. I tried to get into everything that unfolded, but the guy was too aggressive, and I quickly felt queasy with shame. I was relieved when we finally put our clothes on and went back to the party.

7/6

I had the sudden realization on our way to Youngstown that we were on the last leg of our trip, and I started feeling emo about it. Jason bought a pack of cigarettes at a gas station and asked if he could smoke while he drove.

"Go for it," I said.

"Last night was gnarly," he said after taking a long drag.

"Yeah, it was intense."

He narrowed his eyes as he let smoke stream from his mouth. I wondered if he'd pushed me out of my comfort zone intentionally, if he wanted me to get scared and shy away from him so I would finally make up my mind and quit fucking with his emotions.

We got to Youngstown too early for the session at Section 8, so we went to Tim's place, who Jason knew from his FBM trip. His apartment was flooded with empty beer cans and greasy Little Caesar's boxes, some of which still had slices of pizza in them. I could see why Tim and the FBM dudes got along so well. He chugged an entire forty before we went to the skatepark. I had no idea how people could ride like that, or why they'd want to. Riding was enough of an escape in itself.

I'd been to Section 8 a few other times, but it blew me away all over again. There were individual sections, but you could transfer in and out of each to ride the entire park, which was huge. Jason did that massive transfer from the bowl to the mini Nate Wessel did in the Square One video—but he actually nosed it into the transition.

We went back to Tim's place, where we were crashing. He invited people over, and it was the typical scenario of ten guys trying to hit on three girls. Tim wouldn't leave two of them alone. He was older and stout, with neck tattoos and gauged ears. I used to think girls had it easy in those situations, since they could pick whomever they wanted. But that was obviously bullshit when they were completely outnumbered and the hunger from dudes was so relentless.

Tim eventually wore the girls down and got them to go into his room to smoke a bowl. He stepped out after a while to pour some rum and Cokes. Thinking no one was watching, or that no one would care, he pulled out a tiny plastic baggie with white powder from his pants pocket and sprinkled it into two of the drinks. I hesitated but knew I couldn't let him go through with it.

"What the fuck are you doing?" I said, staring daggers at him.

"Oh, we're just doing some Molly. I already took mine. Want some?"

"Bullshit. You're spiking their drinks."

He put his hands up like the accusation was out of left field. "What? You're crazy, dude."

Jason had been talking/flirting with a guy in the corner. "What's up, Ry?" he said. "Everything good?"

"This rapist asshole is trying to pull some shit."

Tim was still putting on the bewildered act. "Your friend needs to chill," he told Jason.

"I saw him slip something into those drinks."

Without even considering I was telling the truth, Jason said, "Are you kidding me, Ry? We're on this again?"

"Why would I make it up?"

Jason looked at Tim and then back at me, unsure what to do. I went with my gut impulse and walked into Tim's room. "I saw that asshole slip something in your drinks," I told the girls. "I'd leave if I was you."

Considering the way he'd been acting, they didn't question what I said. The girl with two lip rings flipped Tim off and said, "Fuck you, you creep piece of shit." They both got up from his bed, got their friend in the living room, and left, despite his pleas for them to stay.

Tim immediately got in my face. "You little pussy. You come to my place and pull that shit?"

"You're being a little bitch, Ry," Jason said. "You have to stop with this bullshit."

Without thinking twice, I reared back and slugged Tim in the jaw. More surprised than hurt, he paused for a second before grabbing me by the throat.

Jason quickly broke us up and shoved me toward the door. "Get the fuck out of here," he said.

Not needing to be told twice, I left, went downstairs, and got in my truck. I could hear Jason and Tim yelling, but I couldn't make out what *they were saying. I sat there for at least an hour, staring at the apartment door and hoping Jason would come out before I finally fell into a fitful sleep.*

7/7

I woke up early, chilled from sleeping in my truck. I thought about leaving Jason. Instead, I went upstairs and pounded on the door. When Tim answered, he looked half-dead from partying the night before. His eyes had a yellow tinge, and his skin was gray. "You here for your little girlfriend?"

"Just tell Jason we're leaving."

"You're lucky he saved you last night," *Tim said, flicking his cigarette between drags.* "I would've destroyed you."

There was no point in responding, so I just turned around and walked downstairs. Jason came down after fifteen minutes. He got in the truck without saying anything or looking at me.

Needing coffee and food before leaving Youngstown, I went to Burger King. Jason didn't answer when I asked if he wanted anything, so I ordered for him, knowing what he usually got there. Waiting in the drive-thru line, I lost it. "Seriously, J, you know Tim is a sack of shit. I saw what I saw—and I guarantee you that's not the first time he's done something like that."

"You're blowing it way out of proportion, like always. You don't know what was happening. You always assume the absolute worst about people."

"He might as well have 'Rapist' tattooed on his forehead."

"Frank and Devin have known him forever. He and those girls were doing Molly together. You don't know what you're talking about."

I was about to respond, but the car ahead of us pulled up. I paid, got our food and coffee, then drove off, immediately picking up the argument. "J, I've been trying to tell you, seriously, Devin is a sick fuck. We were just kids when he brought us into all that shit."

"You're going to try telling me you didn't want to? Give me a fucking break, Ry. Devin is a good friend. He loves both of us. The holier-than-thou routine with you has gotten out of hand. I know Natalie loves it, but I see through it."

I realized how tightly I was gripping the steering wheel and tried to cool off. "I'm worried about you," I told him. "You're better than those guys."

"Worry about yourself."

We ate without saying anything. We drove to Pittsburgh, where we were planning to ride trails with Chris Doyle and Brandon Pundai. I turned on my blinker to take the exit to their jumps, but Jason said, "Fuck it. Let's just go home."

The drive home was tense and airless. When I pulled up to the Cutlass in Philly, which was parked in my spot at the apartment, Jason got out and put his stuff in his car. He looked at me like he was about to say something but then drove off.

∿

That evening, I curled up on the couch and watched TV, clutching a pillow to my chest. It killed me to think about how Jason and I might be done with each other—certainly on a romantic level, but now it seemed like our friendship might be impossible to maintain as well, which hurt even more.

Waking up the next day, I was never surer of what I wanted. I called Natalie and asked if she wanted to come over.

"Let's just talk on the phone," she said. "You know things won't just magically go back to how they were, right?"

"I can wait as long as it takes," I said. "You're it for me."

"…I hope that's true. I can't be your second choice."

"I can't imagine going through life with anyone else."

She asked about the trip. I didn't hold back because I wanted to be fully honest with her. After telling her about the party in

Chicago, I said, "If you want to fuck someone else, go for it. For real. It would be totally fair."

She paused for a few seconds before responding. "I made out with two guys and did some other stuff with another one, but it didn't feel that great, not like it does with you."

I was mad but knew I had no right to be, not after my escapades. Knowing full well what a trip with Jason entailed, Natalie took her chance to test different waters. "Fuck those guys," I said, half-jokingly.

"Want their info so you can go beat their asses?" Her smartass laugh sent tingles down my spine. "You could join a cool hardcore crew afterward."

I told her about catching Tim trying to drug those girls' drinks and having a blowout with Jason over it.

"Oh my God, you're serious?"

"I called the dude out and punched him, then they kicked me out, so I slept in my truck. Jason and I barely talked on the drive home. I don't get why he defends such pieces of shit."

"Just give him time," she said. "He's smarter than those assholes. He just needs to realize it."

As if trying to convince myself, I said, "I think I'm done with him." But as soon as I got off the phone, I started writing about our trip. It was my way of staying connected to Jason.

36

I was in class when I got Devin's call. As my phone vibrated in my pocket, I thought it was either my mom or a telemarketer calling. It had been two months since Jason and I went on our trip—and we still hadn't talked. Natalie and I had just begun our junior year. We were unofficially back together, but we were taking it slow. As soon as I heard Devin's message saying, "Get up here to St. Luke's. Jason's in a fucking coma," I cursed myself for listening to my blowhard psychology professor give his lecture instead of taking the call. Devin was scared shitless when I got ahold of him.

I called Laurie on my way to Bethlehem, not knowing the full story myself.

She freaked out and yelled, "What the fuck happened to my son?" I told her I'd call as soon as I found out.

My fight with Jason had already been playing on a loop in my head. As I looked for a parking spot at the hospital, it was all I could think about. I knew I was right to stop Tim, but guilt still clawed at my stomach. What if the last time Jason and I were ever together, we fought?

Devin and Trevor were waiting in the lobby. They were the last people I wanted to see. Right or wrong, I partly blamed Devin for the rift between Jason and me. But this wasn't the time for drama. They told me how Jason did a turndown over the last jump of a line at Catty, landed at a weird angle, and slammed into a tree at full speed. I'd seen him do every three-sixty variation he could over that jump—perfectly. We could both do turndowns over it in our sleep. It didn't make sense that Jason would wreck so hard on such an easy trick. I wondered if there was something they weren't telling me.

The guy behind the front desk at the hospital told me it was family only in Jason's room. "He's my brother." I said it with enough conviction for him not to question it.

I wish I didn't remember it all in such crushing detail: the quiet-but-persistent electronic beeps; the unnatural air sounds of the machine helping Jason breathe; the tube shoved down his throat and the IV in his arm; the chemical smell of the sterilized room; the numb glare of the fluorescent lights; the thin cotton of his hospital gown; his swollen lips, cheek, and nose; the yellowed beginnings of a bruise that covered the entire left side of his face; the stark quiet of him not talking shit.

I called Laurie again and told her everything I knew. I can't imagine how excruciating the drive from Suffield must've been for her. When she got to the hospital, she looked at me like she might slap me before going over to Jason and telling him he was going to wake up. He didn't have a choice. He was all she had.

PART THREE
The Dirt in Our Skin

37

I'll probably always remember the two weeks and three days Jason was in his coma as one of the most agonizing times of my life. Every time my phone buzzed, I thought it was Laurie about to tell me that he'd died or woken up. I was in this horrible existential vice from the moment I woke up to when I finally fell asleep. I couldn't stop thinking about how, if our fight was the last time we talked, I wouldn't be able to forgive myself.

I went to see him as often as I could. Natalie came with me most times. We'd sit and read the assigned books from our Romantic lit course aloud because the nurses said hearing people talk might help Jason. It was the only way I could even half pay attention to that stuff. I also read from my psych and sociology textbooks, letting the dry, clinical language put me to sleep, if only for an hour. When we were alone, I held Jason's hand and told him I was sorry. I told him I loved him.

Most of the Little Devil team who lived on the East Coast visited. Frank from FBM and some of those dudes came out, too. Part of me thought that since Jason was riding for the company, Frank should be footing the hospital bill. (This was before people could stay on their parents' insurance until they're twenty-six, so it was all uninsured.) I also knew that Frank barely scraped by with enough money to pay rent for his tiny apartment in Binghamton, that he paid his riders their (small) paychecks before buying groceries for himself. Even for riders sponsored by bigger companies, that's typically how it was in BMX: if you got hurt, you were on your own.

Laurie told her boss she wouldn't be back until Jason woke up. The hospital staff got to know her, me, and Natalie by name. Laurie would sit and stare at her son, silently but viscerally willing him to wake up. I'd always considered myself a realist and hated self-help mantras. But I started to understand the appeal when Jason was in his coma. You couldn't let yourself think he would die because the thought would eat you alive.

∿

When he finally woke up, it was the opposite of the night-and-day transition you see on made-for-TV movies and soap operas, where the person wakes up from a coma and immediately goes back to normal.

Jason tentatively blinked open his eyes.

I'd fallen asleep in the dingy gray hospital chair with the metal bar that pinched your back. I was jolted awake by Laurie. Jason seemed to look at her, but, with his clouded eyes and distant pupils, it was hard to tell what he registered, if anything. This was not the momentary daze of someone waking up from a nap. He'd fallen into the void, and it was clear, even though I desperately hoped otherwise, it would be a long time before he climbed out.

When I told Laurie I was paying for the medical bills with the money Dad had saved for me to buy a house, she said, "Are you out of your fucking mind? I can't let you do that, Ry."

The decision was already made, I told her. Dad suggested it himself before I had the chance to ask.

∿

You probably want the list: cracked skull, broken jaw, sinuses, and nose. Four knocked-out teeth. Separated shoulder. Tracheotomy. Feeding tubes. Hemiparesis on the left side of his body. He had to relearn how to eat and walk.

I knew I'd ride again at some point, but while Jason was in the hospital, it was the last thing I wanted to do. I started keeping a journal for him. I had to believe the day would come when he would want to read all of it and remember how far he'd come.

10/8

Today was the first time I heard you speak since you woke up. It was more like a murmur. I've never wanted to hear you talk shit more in my life. I can't stop thinking about our fight. I hate myself for it.

10/10

They removed your tracheal tube earlier today. You have a large hole in the middle of your neck that's covered by a square bandage. Your hair is longer than I've seen it in quite a while, and you have this skeevy facial hair. I said you look like shit, but I couldn't tell if you knew I was joking. I said sorry and that you actually look pretty hessian.

10/18

I'm watching a nurse teach you how to chew. I hate that BMX caused this.

10/23

You can eat soft food on your own, but you need help if it involves a utensil. They have a soft-serve machine in the cafeteria, so I got you a huge swirl. When I fed it to you, your eyes lit up.

10/31

You're starting to track people more when they come in. Your eyes are still puffy, but the rest of the swelling on your face has gone down. A few of the Posh guys came by and told you they love you.

Laurie plays Zeppelin and Skynyrd records for you, and I play Johnny Cash, Hank Williams, and Elliott Smith, the last because I know you love his music but would never admit it. You mouthed some of the words to "Tuesday's Gone," that Skynyrd song we used to make fun of. I told you it was Halloween. You asked if I was going trick or treating.

11/18

You're starting to move more. It seems like shifting to look around is less painful. You can feed yourself as long as it's something you can eat with just your right hand. You can move the fingers on your left hand and wiggle the toes on your left foot. They told me and your mom you'll most likely be able to walk again, but not to get our hopes up for much else. It fucked me up to think you'd never ride again, that the world would be robbed of that gift.

All the nurses and doctors say how strong you are, how hard you're pushing, especially when we can't see it. I'm sure they say that to everyone, but I also know you're a tough fucker.

11/20

My mom and dad came to see you. I guess things have gotten a bit better between them because they were able to drive down together. They brought Arby's milkshakes and those Jell-O half-and-half puddings because they know you love them. Before they left, you looked Dad in the eyes and said, "I'm worried about Ry. Make sure you take care of him." We all broke down.

12/15

You've been doing elastic band exercises with the nurses and physical therapist to regain movement in your left arm. I'm prouder of you for each inch of progress than I have been for anything you've done on a bike. If you can ride again, I wonder if you'll even want to.

You're on a constant stream of pain medication, and there are dark circles around your eyes. Your skin is the palest I've ever seen. These have been the longest months of my life. Each day is like getting a tooth pulled without anesthesia.

12/18

Devin visited with Chris Stauffer and Garrett Byrnes. You were in a room with your heroes, and it was obvious how much they respect you. Sometimes I see this dejected anger on your face that scares the hell out of me. There was none of that today.

I want nothing to do with Devin, but this was obviously not the time or place to start shit with him or you. For now, you and I will have to agree to disagree about him and leave it there. He's not worth being at odds with you.

After they left, I told you how much I regretted our fight on the last day of our trip. "I'm sorry that's how it ended."

"Brothers can fight," you said.

12/24

Rob sent you an early edit of Old Glory for Christmas. We're the only people besides him who've seen it. You have the last part. The last part in a video with the best trail riders in the world. It's the most beautiful riding I've ever seen. After we watched it, you started making plans for the trips we're going to take when you get out of this shithole.

12/31

We're on Christmas break, so Natalie and I are with you pretty much constantly, unless she has a shift at the bookstore. Sometimes Harold comes with us. When you first saw how long his hair has gotten, you laughed and said, "You look like a dirty reprobate, Harry. Now come here and give us a kiss."

Your mom is here every weekend, starting on Friday nights. She was originally going to transfer you to Saint Francis in Suffield, but she thinks you're in better hands here. Plus, she knows I can spend more time with you than she can. This way, you have someone around more.

I've been reading this book to you about skateboarding called The Answer Is Never. *You're picking up more of it than I expected. The writer talks a lot about how skating permanently shapes your perception of the world, how a rail or ledge is never just a rail or ledge again once you know you can skate it. The same thing obviously applies to BMX. It's the first time I've wanted to ride since your crash.*

1/30

You've been working up to it all month with the physical therapist and nurses, but you were able to hold yourself up enough in a walker to take small steps with your right foot and hold your left foot off the ground. You were completely spent afterward. I'm trying to stay positive, but it feels like we'll never leave, like we've been here forever.

2/18

You've been taking little steps in the walker with your left foot. Today the PT had you kick a beach ball forward as you walked. You were stoked on it for a while, but then that dejection came crashing down. When we were alone, you said, "What the fuck will I do if I can't ride anymore?" I said you'd be able to, that the doctors kept saying how fast you're recovering.

You just said, "They don't know shit."

2/27

We were listening to Elliott Smith when you said, "I don't want to hear this emo bullshit anymore, Ry. Put on some Eyehategod." So we listened to Eyehategod. You kept asking me to turn it up. You closed your eyes and looked at peace while the ugly sludge played. When I left that night, the nurses looked at me like I'd wiped poop on the walls.

3/5

You turned twenty-one today. I bought an ice cream cake at Baskin Robbins, and you destroyed it. It's awesome to see your appetite come back. I have no idea how your mom did it, but she got you an autographed Eyehategod record. It has a personal note from the band: "To Jason, Get well soon so you can help us burn everything down." I kept asking Laurie how she'd gotten ahold of them. She smiled wryly and shook her head, thinking it was funny not to tell me.

3/18

Since February, the doctors have been saying you'll be out soon, so it eventually stopped meaning anything. Apparently, it's real now. You keep saying this place feels like a prison.

3/24

Holy fuck. They gave you a discharge date. Part of me doesn't want to count on it too much, but I wasn't going to be a dick and ruin the moment. You wanted to celebrate, so I bought another ice cream cake. We ate it while listening to Master of Puppets *at a rude volume. The metal head nurse you love came in and rocked out with us for a few minutes before turning the boom box down herself.*

4/2

You walked out of that shithole with me helping only a tiny bit. Your mom took you back to Suffield. I've never been happier for you, but all I could think about when I got home was how I wouldn't get to see you as much. I felt unanchored until Natalie said, "Why don't you go ride?" I went to FDR even though it was the middle of the day. I felt a bit uneasy at first but then got pissed and started roasting. None of the skaters said anything.

38

I took an Intro to Creative Nonfiction class during the spring when Jason was in the hospital. From the first lecture on, I knew the teacher was going to piss me off. With his quaffed hair and unironic sporting of tweed jackets, I could tell Dr. Lundgren (he insisted we call him doctor) was the type of person who thought writing had to be dense and obtuse to be good. He looked at me like I'd pissed on his shoes when I said, about a David Foster Wallace essay, "Doesn't it feel like he's just constantly trying to show off how smart he is?" I ended up coming around a bit after reading his cruise ship essay about American entitlement and despair, but, to me, DFW came off like a stunt rider who tries too hard.

One good thing about constantly visiting Jason in the hospital was that I had a ton of time to do homework. I read everything for all my classes. I worked on my first workshop essay for three weeks, adding and taking things away every day. I pulled together bits and pieces from *Tapping the Source*, *The Answer is Never*, and *Dogtown and Z-Boys* to make a case for riding as an art form. I included scenes of Jason and me riding trails, pools, and full-pipes, and I read it to him to make sure I got it right.

Lundgren usually let students drive the workshop until the end, when he gifted us with his profound verdict on why the writing didn't work. But during my workshop, he started out. "I'll cut right to it. Does anyone else find it ridiculous that grown men popping wheelies on children's bikes could be considered art?" The little Ivy League wannabes nodded and raised their hands to say the same thing in slightly altered language.

You weren't supposed to talk when your writing got workshopped. Before I had time to think about it, I was standing up and saying, "What makes you, Professor Chuckle Fuck, an art expert? Because you've wasted so many years hiding in ivory towers?" I realized as soon as I said it that I'd overreacted.

I'd never gotten kicked out of class before, but there I was: kicked the fuck out.

I picked up Natalie from the bookstore, and we went to see Jason in Bethlehem. Part of her loved this escapade, but she also worried I'd get permanently kicked out of Lundgren's class, which I needed to take that semester in order to graduate on time. And she was right. I really had to grovel and act repentant when I went to see Lundgren in his office.

"This is not how people act in academia," he said, crossing his leg over the other. A large Chuck Close print hung on the wall behind his desk, upon which several stacks of ungraded papers sat. "We're supposed to have civilized discourse."

His condescending tone irked me, but I just said, "Yes, sir. I'm so sorry, Professor."

"For the record, I hope you know I was playing devil's advocate. You can't be so sensitive."

I thought about telling him that my best friend was, at that exact moment, relearning how to use his body and mind, that we'd sacrificed more for riding than he would for anything in his cushy, terrified life. Instead, I nodded and asked him to sign the form that would let me back into his class.

I was supposed to let it go. But I didn't. Instead of choosing a less-heated topic, I wrote my second essay as a continuation of the first. This time, I pulled in all this material about dance, which, next to surfing and skating, was the best way I could explain the artfulness of riding: dancers sacrificed their bodies for fleeting moments of beauty, and their art revolved around physicality. I went deeper in my skating research, pulling in quotes from Rodney Mullen when he talked about the evolution of skating as a process of creating a new language, a new vernacular, to describe all the possible variations of movement. I combined that with these little meditations on communing with the dirt and woods, how our jumps became expressions that lay somewhere between nature and thought. I brought the blues into it, talking about how the best players conveyed a depth of emotion and personal identity by playing the same notes as everyone else, just like the best riders injected feeling into tricks that had been done countless times before. I wrote about how people like Jason, Aitken, Chase Hawk, and Garrett Byrnes imbued their energy into basic maneuvers, so each one became an extension of themselves. I wanted to make the essay as unfuckwithable as a well-built brick wall—and I wanted to smash Lundgren's face into it.

It ended up being the only essay that semester he didn't completely dismantle. All he said at the end of my workshop was, "You'll never convince me that BMX is on the same level as writing, film, or visual art, but I suppose this is as good of a case as one could make."

I shouldn't have said it, but I did: "I'd argue with you if I thought your opinion was worth a shit. But thanks for the feedback."

His face turned red, but he didn't kick me out. We were both glad not to see each other's mug anymore when the class ended.

39

I completed my student assistantship at the JJC that summer. In May, Natalie and I moved into a studio apartment near Fitler Square with a one-year lease, which would take us through our senior year. Harold and I still got along, but he wasn't going to complain about getting our apartment to himself. His parents could easily afford it.

Busy with moving and getting settled in, I wasn't able to make it up to Suffield as often as I would've liked. Meanwhile, Jason was progressing at what seemed like a mind-blowing pace. In the hospital, I tried to take his recovery on its own terms instead of predicting specific outcomes. I was still trying to approach it from that angle—mentally preparing myself for the worst—but there was no need. By July, Jason was walking, jogging a bit, and spending two hours each day pedaling a stationary bike. It was almost enough to make me believe in a higher power. Almost.

When I went home in August, I drove straight to Jason's house, parked, and rang the doorbell. Then I heard a freewheel ticking in the driveway. "I'm right here, ya fuckin' pirate," Jason said, riding past me. It was the first time I'd ever seen him wear a helmet to pedal around. But we would've been fools not to wear helmets all the time after his crash. We were fools not to wear them before. Once you saw someone as naturally gifted as Jason get injured like that, you couldn't escape the reality that it could happen to you at any time. Jason's wreck also got several pros we knew to start wearing helmets, even on street, which was previously considered one of the biggest stylistic faux pas.

"Check this out," Jason said before doing a little bunny hop and then a short manual.

I'm sure it would've looked insignificant to anyone else. To me, it was Michael Jordan returning to the Bulls after his year of baseball, the year when no one knew if he'd play basketball again. Actually, it was way better than that. It was Jason back on his bike.

Within another month, he was doing solid manuals and one-eighties on flat ground. By the end of fall, he was riding small jumps and pumping around at skateparks. He eventually got a lot more back, but there was always this slight uncertainty in his body after the crash, like the knowledge of what could happen had suffused his cells. He was riding, though—and yes, it was beautiful.

Since Natalie wanted to focus on her graduate school applications that fall, she was eager for me to visit Suffield as often as possible. One weekend at my dad's house, I noticed a handful of different-colored AA tokens on the kitchen counter. He saw me looking at them.

"I see Laurie at every meeting. I used to think it was bullshit," he said, putting his hands in his jeans pockets. "But there's something to that fellowship stuff. Those people actually care about you. I've slipped up a few times, but they always welcome me back." He was cleanly shaven. I was still trying to get used to his face without the goatee he'd had for as long as I could remember. His chin and cheeks looked soft.

"Fuck yeah, Dad. That's great."

He paused for a moment, then said, "I wish I could take it back, the way I acted."

"I know."

Jason and I began fixing our jumps. He made sure to come inside Dad's house every time we went out there. He was chipping away at a calcified fossil, each time knocking loose some of the unease between us and my dad. While Jason was in the hospital, we'd developed an unspoken understanding that we were better off as friends than romantic partners. Our road trip had shown us that our friendship was fragile, and we needed to protect it.

Digging, Jason would get spent pretty quickly. I knew better than to baby him. We got Battery up and running, although it was too gnarly for him at that point. So we started building Beholder, a mid-sized line that would make me think of the way ospreys glide above the surface of the water, nonchalantly cruising.

Jason didn't do tricks much anymore; he just enjoyed the feeling of putting life on pause while in the air. Our woods felt so goddamn tranquil. I'd almost forgotten how much I loved it when there was no sound besides the searing zip of our tires on packed dirt, the soft rustle of leaves and branches, and whatever birds and animals were around. Part of me would always be at Posh. But this was home.

The first jump of Beholder

40

Natalie, the genius, ended up getting into nearly every master's program she applied to, including Harvard and Columbia. She'd tear open the letters and try to get me to dance around with her, her feet clomping on the weathered hardwood floor of our apartment. I was proud but not at all surprised. Brown offered her the best deal, with teaching, full tuition remission, and a decent stipend. While she'd wanted to avoid the rich-kids-in-a-vacuum Ivy League experience for her bachelor's degree, Temple wasn't rigorous enough for Natalie. She wanted more of a challenge.

Just weeks before graduation, I saw an ad for a teaching job at the JJC in Hartford. I had exactly the experience they were looking for, although they were skeptical at the interview when I told them I specifically wanted to teach incarcerated youth. Natalie and I found a rental house for dirt cheap in a quiet small town called Windham, splitting the distance between Providence and Hartford.

Bands like Glassjaw and From Autumn to Ashes had told me that strain in relationships was almost always the woman's fault. But it was obvious that the tension between me and Natalie derived from my uncertainty and lack of control. Part of me still held on to the idea of having a polyamorous relationship with her and Jason, but I knew Natalie fulfilled something deeper within me than Jason could. If I wanted to be with her, I had to let it go. Natalie knew I struggled, but she trusted me not to act on my urges—and I never wanted to fuck things up with her again. As for our actual fights, we usually retreated to different parts of the house until we were ready to talk. The time apart during our break made us sure that we didn't want to live without each other.

So there was our new life, with Natalie teaching precocious undergrads, going to literature seminars, writing dense scholarly essays about semiotics and postcolonialism, and talking shit about various professors and members of her cohort. We started going to these awful faculty parties in Providence. Natalie thought it was hilarious to watch me squirm at those things. As people droned on and on about whatever mess of abstractions they were obsessed with, I desperately hoped someone would pop out from behind a house plant and shoot off a Roman candle.

I started teaching surly kids in my own classroom at the Hartford JJC. These were the children of Ocean Vuong's Hartford in *On Earth We're Briefly Gorgeous*—kids who, for the most part, got in trouble for defying, or simply living within, a system designed to oppress and destroy them. I sometimes came across the occasional middle- to upper-middle-class white kid, but they were few and far between in there. Many of the youth at least partially warmed to me when they saw that I genuinely gave a shit about them getting better at reading and writing during our time together. I helped a few students get their GEDs while locked up, and I showed many others that literature can be a haven for people with bodies and backgrounds like theirs. Despite my best efforts, I also fucked up and tripped over my whiteness and privilege like untied shoelaces, whether it was in the form of mispronouncing names that didn't look like mine or assigning work that caused students pain in ways I didn't foresee. I learned from my mistakes and did my best not to repeat them. There were also these horrible moments of powerlessness when I knew one of the youth was getting tortured by another kid, or, more often, a group of kids. Trying to make them stop usually only made it worse and more clandestine, which was a hard pill to swallow. I'd get pissed at them, but then, when we were in the classroom together, I mainly thought about how they were reenacting their own trauma. There were no easy answers in those situations. You did what you could.

I sometimes dreamt of the overlooked genius who'd go on to write the next *Citizen*, but I tried to find more motivation in the small but powerful moments when I noticed someone's reading and writing had gotten better, if only incrementally. It helped get the youth on my side when they found out they could cuss in my classroom, as long as it wasn't threatening or degrading. We dropped a shitload of f-bombs, and we didn't read bullshit like *The Scarlet Letter*.

∿

That first fall we lived in Windham, Jason and I finished Beholder, which we named after the third song on...*And Justice For All*. It was pretty straightforward—five chin-height jumps with a berm in the middle and a hip at the end—but that was the beauty of it. We took great care to make the tops of the lips and landings perfectly level, shaving the sides so the jumps had that sleek look you want. I was about to give it the first test run, but Jason walked his bike to the top and beat me to it. He simply flowed, doing subtle, graceful whips. His freewheel reverberated in the trees, a buzzsaw yawp.

Jason riding Beholder

41

My stomach dropped when Jason said, "Hey, Ry," with a rare look of dead seriousness. He stuck his shovel in the ground and leaned against it. "I want you to meet my boyfriend."

"Jesus fuck, dude, I thought you were going to tell me your mom has cancer or some shit." A bolt of jealousy shot through me even though I knew it was inevitable that Jason would end up with someone else. I wanted him to be happy, so the envy made me feel like a selfish ass. I tried not to let it show.

Jason loosened up and told me about Keith, running all his sentences together with an infectious giddiness. "He does amateur wrestling and listens to bands like Floor and Weedeater. He's not just a bear, he's a fucking grizzly."

"He sounds rad, J. We'll have dinner with Natalie."

When Keith walked into our house with Jason later that week, I thought, *Holy shit, he is a grizzly*. He had a thick handlebar mustache, and, even through his Carhartt jacket, you could tell how huge his arms and chest muscles were. Part of me was genuinely stoked for Jason—the other part was a swamp of envy and shame.

Keith wrestled by night and did technical writing for a software company by day. If that doesn't sound like the coolest person in the world, I don't know what to tell you. It didn't hurt that Keith was wearing a Crowbar beanie the first time he came over.

As I cleaned crusty tomato sauce out of the casserole dish that night, Natalie said, "I can't believe it. Keith already feels like family."

Snuggled up to her in bed that night, I wondered if Keith was better for Jason than I ever would have been. I ruminated on the thought until I finally fell asleep, breathing Natalie in.

∿

Keith had told us about his wrestling persona, but Natalie and I had to see it in person to fully appreciate it. I'd never been to an amateur wrestling match and didn't know what to expect. It was in an old basketball gym—and yes, there were mullets, not to mention enough camouflage to make it near impossible to see anyone. It had that down-to-earth feel I've always loved about BMX jams. The people in attendance and classic rock blasting from the speakers immediately told me I was going to love this. I bought a Snickers for me and a Coke for Natalie from the sparsely toothed man working the concession stand.

Keith used Pantera's "Cowboys From Hell" for his intro music. The crowd booed as he strutted through the doors and the announcer said, "Ladies and gentlemen, it's Pebbles, the world's most ravishing redneck." Keith was wearing a trucker hat that said "Wine 'em/ Dine 'em/ 69 'em" and beat-up overalls with no shirt underneath. Once in the ring, he took off the overalls to reveal hot pink spandex. He shook his ass, and the crowd booed some more.

He was matched up against The Patriot, who wore American flag spandex and boots. As they egged each other on, exchanged slaps, threw each other into the ropes, and performed acrobatics that didn't seem possible for such big dudes, I remember thinking, *Holy shit. It's low-brow Shakespeare.*

∿

I hadn't hung out with Keith without Jason, so I was surprised to see his name pop up on my phone. It had been about three months since we'd met.

"Hey, Ryan, you got a minute?" He told me Jason had been falling into more of those depressive funks where he'd sulk and get bitingly negative about everything. Laurie had told me about them as well. I'd heard Jason get down on himself a few times, saying his riding was a joke compared to what it used to be, that he might as well quit. A veil seemed to fall over the world during those moments. He knew I'd make him get help if it kept happening, so he hid it from me. He'd experienced multiple dizzy spells at the jumps, putting his bike or shovel down and leaning against a tree until it passed. He suffered from some memory loss as well, occasionally making a joke or observation and then repeating it a few minutes later.

The next time we were digging, I said, "If you're still getting depressed, you have to get help. You can't pretend it's not there."

"Keith told you? What the fuck, man?"

"He loves you, dipshit."

When Keith caught Jason sneaking extra pain pills, he, Laurie, and I went to some NA meetings with Jason. It eventually stopped. As he listened to people's stories about how opioids had ravaged their lives, Jason looked horrified, like he was watching someone get buried alive.

After that, there was no question. Keith was family.

∿

X Games came to Boston, so Jason, Keith, Natalie, and I made the trip. As much as Jason and I talked shit on stunt riders, you couldn't really deny how gnarly it was, especially when seeing it in person. I'd never seen a BMX contest in a stadium, so it was strange to watch riders spin, flip, and crash on the jumbotron—and with corporate ads plastered everywhere. We knew a bunch of people there, so it was like a family reunion with everyone seeing Jason. Multiple riders teared up when they saw how well he was doing. He was still dealing with fallout from his head injury—and likely would be for the rest of his life—but he was lucky compared to most other riders who'd survived severe brain trauma.

Devin and his crew built the dirt course, which was just a straightforward six pack so riders could huck triple tailwhips, frontflip variations, backflip double tailwhips, and the like. It wasn't a failure of imagination on Devin's part. That's just what the higher-ups always wanted for X Games: three straight jumps.

Over the years, I'd tried to keep my distance from Devin. It was hard because we saw him around all the time, obviously at Posh and Catty, but also at Incline Club, the Little Devil warehouse, PennSkate, and FDR. My vibe toward him had changed, though, and he knew it. We kept it cordial but didn't interact much. Jason, on the other hand, had never stopped looking up to him, and I understood it: he was one of the most skilled trail builders in the world. We'd both passed him up on a riding level, but the way he designed and built jumps still had an otherworldly tinge—when he wasn't working for X Games, that is.

"Devin!" Jason yelled when he saw him milling about in a crowd of riders and industry people near the street course. We walked up to him. "I want you to meet my boyfriend, Keith."

"Your *boyfriend?*" Devin said, his lips curling into his signature shit-eating grin.

"That's funny?" Keith said, staring through him.

"No, no, man, not at all. I'm happy for Jason, is all."

I'd never seen Devin look so small. That's the last time Jason or I talked to him.

~~~

Keith and Jason got married about one month before my daughter, Analise, was born. It was actually a civil union, but none of us used that phrase.

Natalie and I found out we were having a girl just a few weeks after Jason told me Keith had popped the question—and he'd said yes.

"Are you excited to have a daughter?" Natalie asked on our way home from the ultrasound appointment.

She and I had gotten married a year earlier. Before we started planning, I thought she might want a courthouse wedding. To my surprise, she wanted to go all out, which was awesome—because I did, too. We got married at the Fenway Garden Society in Boston in May. There was a drizzling rain at the beginning, but it cleared up into a sunny, vibrantly green day. Natalie wore a white dress with blue accents and a platinum, diamond-encrusted nose ring I'd bought her. She seemed to glow. I wore a black suit, gray shirt, and leather Vans slip-ons. Jason was my best man.[5] Natalie's best friend, Sarah, led the ceremony. We wrote each other letters instead of regular vows and read them aloud. For the reception, we'd found a caterer who could serve a mish-mash of Japanese and American dishes. I ate a huge burger and a shitload of sushi, and Natalie had udon noodles with a chocolate shake and a side of onion rings.

"Yeah, of course," I said. "I'm also scared, to be honest."

She laughed. "Why scared?"

"Scared I'll fuck up. Scared of the world we live in."

"Just make sure you listen."

Between runs at our jumps the following Saturday, I told Jason that Natalie and I'd found out we were having a girl.

---

5   When he realized he was supposed to plan my bachelor party, Jason asked if I wanted to go to a Chippendales show in New York. We rode Posh instead.

"Fuck yeah!" he said, giving me a hug. "I was actually hoping it's a girl."

We took a few more laps before I asked him if he was inviting my dad to his wedding.

"We're getting married at the house. Didn't he tell you?"

Dad spent the next four months building a gorgeous black walnut altar. It was a small, two-step pedestal with enough room for three people. On the side, he carved Jason and Keith's initials inside small sprockets. We strung up white Christmas lights and set up a bunch of chairs and tables in the backyard the day before the ceremony. Natalie was very pregnant, but she still helped, even though Dad, Laurie, and I repeatedly told her there was no need. Harold, who I hadn't seen in more than a year, showed up with his girlfriend. His dark brown hair completely covered his shoulders, and he had the beginnings of a tattoo sleeve of psychedelic computer circuitry on his left arm.

Next to mine and Natalie's, it was the raddest wedding I've ever attended. Keith and Jason walked the aisle to an old Hank Williams song. Looking at them in their brand-new slip-ons and black blazers with camo button-down shirts underneath, I felt like a narcissistic jackass for ever getting jealous of their relationship. Keith's sister led the ceremony. I was Jason's best man. The air was heavy with summertime humidity. Sweat poured down our faces.

For dinner, there was a buffet of Doritos Locos tacos, chalupas, and supreme burritos. We listened to Eyehategod and drank Mountain Dew from champagne flutes. Throughout the day and into the evening, Dad somehow kept it civil with Mom's new boyfriend, Tom, although you could see in his neck how tense he was. Laurie was beaming as she walked around with her glass of soda, putting her hand on people's shoulders and laughing.

When they started going out, Jason had been nervous to introduce Keith to Laurie. He hadn't introduced her, or any of us, to someone he was dating before. "What if she doesn't like him?" he asked while we were eating burgers in my truck, exhausted after an evening of digging.

"She's going to like him more than you."

Within weeks, Laurie was calling Keith "Kiki." She started bringing huge signs that said things like "Pebbles 4 President" to his wrestling matches.

Epilogue

She'd only had her training wheels off for three months, but there she was, yelling, "Dad! Look at this wheelie!" And she did it. Analise could now do little wheelies, lifting her front wheel and almost getting a full pedal in. She was four.

We started going to the track soon after. Her full-face helmet looked bigger than she was. You could see this bright purple orb bobbing up and down as she pedaled over the rollers and tabletops. She quickly learned how to pump a bit to gain speed and momentum. I caught glimpses of her cartoonish grin as she pedaled by.

Before Ana could even ride without training wheels, Natalie and I would have long discussions about whether or not we should encourage our daughter to ride BMX. We'd talk about the dangers in sports many parents didn't think twice about exposing their kids to—not just the obvious with football and hockey, but also soccer, basketball, and baseball—any sport where you could get hit in the head with something. And then there was skiing, snowboarding, and surfing. The question became how much risk you were willing to expose your child to, and that's in addition to the daily possibilities of car wrecks, getting hit by a car, or any of the other million things that could kill us in this world. There was self-justification there, sure, but I couldn't deny how much BMX had given me. It was a purpose and identity, which was especially crucial in middle and high school, when that focus anchored me. Jason's wreck had shown us how immense the toll could be—but the reward was immense, too.

Every time Ana crashed, I went through the questioning process again. But I could never break her heart by telling her she couldn't ride anymore. I remembered how small I felt when my dad tried to stop me from doing something I loved, and I never wanted to make Ana feel that way.

Jason and I built a roller line for her at our trails. Jason bought her a kid's shovel and mini wheelbarrow, and she dug with this adorable determination. But you couldn't laugh. It pissed her off. Sometimes, Jason would stare off at the tobacco field or the corrugated warehouse where his family's house and barn once stood—all still owned by Coalition Incorporated. Ana would pull him back to the present moment, though. She was always so jazzed to hang out with him. He could make her laugh harder than anyone else with his rat faces and pirate voice. Watching her ride reminded us both of the magic when we first discovered BMX.

When the roller section was done, her little freewheel buzzed in the tree branches as she pumped through. She walked back up and did it again. And again. And again.

BMX Glossary

Tricks

Bonk: You quickly hit your front or back peg on a ledge, rail, or coping.

Double peg: A grind or stall on both the front and rear pegs, which extend from the wheel axles.

Icepick: A grind or stall on the rear peg.

Invert: You tuck your bike sideways until the wheels go past horizontal and become inverted.

Manual: A wheelie without pedaling.

Tabletop: You tuck your bike into a horizontal position.

Tailwhip: You hold the handlebars while flipping the rest of the bike around one full horizontal rotation with your legs.

Three-sixty: A three-hundred-sixty-degree rotation.

Turndown: You whip your back end to the side and simultaneously turn your handlebars—kind of like a sideways X-up.

Wall-ride: You ride on a wall.

X-up: You turn your front wheel in the air, twisting your arms into an X.

Ramps and jumps

Berm: A curved and embanked turn, like the turns on a NASCAR track.

Coping: The pipe at the top of a ramp's transition that you can grind.

Double: A simple dirt jump with a lip and landing and nothing in the middle.

Full pipe: A full circular tube with transition. You can find them at skateparks and reservoirs.

Half-pipe: A ramp with transition on either side so you can go back and forth.

Lip: The first part of a jump that shoots you in the air.

Quarter pipe: A single transition where you go up, turn around, and come back down. Half of a half-pipe.

Rhythm section: Multiple dirt jumps in a row.

Wall-ride: An embankment leading up to a wall.

Photography Credits

Pg. 31—Mike Szczesny, photo by Christine Szczesny

Pg. 43—Mike Szczesny, photo by Seth Huot

Pg. 49—Photo by Cody Gessel

Pg. 83—Andy Patterson, photo by Ty Stuyvesant

Pg. 87—Mike Szczesny, photo by Seth Huot

Pg. 94—Posh, photo by Zak Yearly

Pg. 96—Eric Jensen, photo by Brian Barnhart

Pg. 97—Mike Aitken and Mike Szczesny, photo by Seth Huot

Pg. 126—Mike Szczesny, photo by Seth Huot

Pg. 136—Mike Szczesny, photo by Steve Buddendeck

Pg. 192—Mike Sczcesny, photo by Kurt Perkins

Pg. 199—Brian Yeagle, photo by Ty Stuyvesant

Pg. 201—Photo by Matt Beringer

Pg. 205—Kurt Perkins, photo by Ty Stuyvesant

Pg. 230—Photo by Mike Szczesny

Pg. 234—Joseph Nazarak, photo by Ty Stuyvesant

Acknowledgments

Remy, Stevie, and Ida, thank you for filling my life with light. I'm the luckiest guy in the world to have such an amazing and inspiring family.

Thanks to the rest of my wonderfully supportive family for everything, now and forever.

Jared, Steve, Bryan, and Paul, thanks for the adventures, laughs, support, forgiveness, and inspiration. TBC will never die. Much love to you and your families.

Jackson Keeler, thank you for believing in this project, helping me shape it, and tirelessly advocating for it.

Hailie Johnson, massive thanks for the astute editorial guidance. You unquestionably made this a better book. Thanks also to Jennifer Psujek for the grammatical eagle eye.

Heartfelt thanks to Tyson Cornell and the rest of the Rare Bird team for making this book a reality. I feel very fortunate to work with you.

Huge thanks to everyone who let me use their amazing photos: Mike Szczesny, Ty Stuyvesant, Seth Huot, Steve Buddendeck, Kurt Perkins, and Matt Beringer.

Last but most definitely not least, endless gratitude for the inspiration: Mike Aitken, Zack Krejmas, Square One, Little Devil, Bojan Louis, sludge metal, Josh Uranker, Jordan Utley, Bike & Trike, style riders, Eric Burns, Morality Crisis, Mike Britson, Oliver

Dammasch, Mike Underdown, Sam Steinberg, Rusty Birdwell, Erin Severson, Denise Pla, John Hales, Chris at Page Against the Machine, *Mid90s*, *Skate Kitchen*, *Minding the Gap*, and kids who build dirt jumps in the woods.